"You come a̶̶̶̶̶̶̶̶̶̶̶̶̶̶ you, don't you? Your body cries out for mine the same way it always did. So why waste it?" Zuhal's voice dipped into a sensual caress. "Why not give in to what we both want—and make love one last and beautiful time?"

Dazedly, Jasmine listened to his arrogant statement—and didn't his attitude justify some of the tough decisions she'd been forced to make? She was about to tell him that it was a mistake to call what he had in mind *making love*, and wondering if he would attempt to persuade her otherwise, when a distant sound changed everything. She moved away from him—not so quickly as to arouse suspicion—praying that Darius was only whimpering in some kind of happy little infant dream and would shortly go back to sleep.

But her prayers went unanswered. The whimpering became louder. It morphed into a cry and then a protesting yell, and she saw Zuhal's face change. Watched the black eyes narrow as his gaze swept questioningly over her, and she quickly stared down at the threadbare rug for fear that he might see the sudden tears welling up in her eyes.

Secret Heirs of Billionaires

There are some things money can't buy...

Living life at lightning pace, these magnates are no strangers to stakes at their highest. It seems they've got it all... That is, until they find out that there's an unplanned item to add to their list of accomplishments!

Achieved:

1. Successful business empire.

2. Beautiful women in their bed.

3. *An heir to bear their name?*

Though every billionaire needs to leave his legacy in safe hands, discovering a secret heir shakes up the carefully orchestrated plan in more ways than one!

Uncover their secrets in:

The Heir the Prince Secures by Jennie Lucas

The Italian's Unexpected Love-Child by Miranda Lee

The Baby the Billionaire Demands by Jennie Lucas

Married for His One-Night Heir by Jennifer Hayward

The Secret Kept from the Italian by Kate Hewitt

Demanding His Secret Son by Louise Fuller

Look out for more stories in the
Secret Heirs of Billionaires series coming soon!

Sharon Kendrick

THE SHEIKH'S SECRET BABY

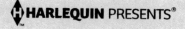

HARLEQUIN PRESENTS®

Recycling programs
for this product may
not exist in your area.

ISBN-13: 978-1-335-53811-6

The Sheikh's Secret Baby

First North American publication 2019

Copyright © 2019 by Sharon Kendrick

Printed in U.S.A.

Sharon Kendrick once won a national writing competition by describing her ideal date: being flown to an exotic island by a gorgeous and powerful man. Little did she realize that she'd just wandered into her dream job! Today she writes for Harlequin, and her books feature often stubborn but always *to-die-for* heroes and the women who bring them to their knees. She believes that the best books are those you never want to end. Just like life...

Books by Sharon Kendrick

Harlequin Presents

A Royal Vow of Convenience
The Italian's Christmas Housekeeper

Conveniently Wed!

Bound to the Sicilian's Bed
The Greek's Bought Bride

One Night With Consequences

Carrying the Greek's Heir
Crowned for the Prince's Heir
Secrets of a Billionaire's Mistress
The Pregnant Kavakos Bride
The Italian's Christmas Secret
Crowned for the Sheikh's Baby

Wedlocked!

The Sheikh's Bought Wife
The Billionaire's Defiant Acquisition

The Billionaire's Legacy

Di Sione's Virgin Mistress

Visit the Author Profile page
at Harlequin.com for more titles.

This book is for Elaine "Lainey" Glasspool, who not only has the sunniest smile, the most Rapunzel-like hair and a spirit of joie de vivre that is positively inspirational—she also knows a wagonload of facts about horses. So thanks for all the equine help, Lainey.

CHAPTER ONE

IT WAS THE LAST place he'd imagined her living. Zuhal frowned. Jasmine? *Here?* In a tiny cottage in the middle of the English countryside, down a lane so narrow it had challenged the progress of his wide limousine? The woman who had loved the sparkle and buzz of the city, hiding herself away in some remote spot. There had to be some kind of mistake.

His frown became a flickering smile of anticipation. Not that he had given a lot of thought to her accommodation. If ever he'd stopped to think about his lusciously proportioned ex-lover—something he tried not to do, for obvious reasons—then it had usually been a predictable flashback to her soft skin. Or the tempting pertness of her breasts. Or the way she used to rain kisses all over his face so that his heart used to punch with pleasure. His groin, too.

He swallowed.

And that, of course, was the reason for his unexpected appearance today. The reason he'd decided to drop in and surprise her.

His throat dried. Why not? He liked sex and so did Jasmine. Of all his lovers, she had been the one who had really lit his fire. Sparks had flown between them from the start and it seemed a pity not to capitalise on that explosive chemistry with a little trip down memory lane. After all, it wasn't as if either of them had entertained any unrealistic expectations. There had been no dreams to be shattered. They hadn't asked for the impossible and had known exactly where the boundaries lay. They had conducted their affair like adults. What possible harm could it do to revisit the past and revel in a little uncomplicated bliss at a time in his life when he needed some light relief like never before?

He felt the smile die on his lips as part of him questioned the sanity of revisiting the past—and a woman—like this. Because he never went back. If you reignited an old relationship, then a woman could almost be excused for thinking it meant more to you than it really did…and no relationship ever meant more than sex to Zuhal Al Haidar.

And since Jazz was realistic enough to accept that, maybe this one time he could be excused for breaking one of his own rules, because destiny was leading him down an unwanted path—a path which had altered his whole future. Silently, he simultaneously cursed and mourned his foolish brother, but all the wishing in the world wasn't going to bring him back, or rewrite the pages of history which had changed his own destiny. He wasn't going to think about that. He was going to concentrate on Jasmine Jones and her soft body. To have her obliterate everything except desire and fulfilment. He was growing hard just thinking about it, because she was the sweetest lover he had ever known.

He stepped over a cracked flagstone, through which a healthy-looking weed was pushing through. It had crossed his mind that she might have replaced him in her affections during the eighteen months they'd been apart, but deep down Zuhal refused to countenance such a scenario—mainly because his ego would not allow him to.

And if she had?

If that were the case, then he would graciously bow out. He was, after all, a desert king, not a savage—even if at times Jazz Jones had possessed the ability to make him feel as primitive as it was possible for a man to feel. He would wish her well and take his pleasure elsewhere, although he couldn't deny he would be disappointed not to revisit her enchanting curves and seeking mouth.

He pushed open the little gate, which even his untrained eye could tell needed a coat of paint, and made a mental note as he walked up the narrow path. Perhaps he would send someone out here to do just that. He lifted the loose door-knocker, which clearly had a screw missing, and frowned. Maybe even get someone to fix that for her, too.

Afterwards.

After he had enjoyed some badly needed solace.

He lifted the knocker, and as it fell heavily against the peeling paintwork he could hear the sound echoing through the tiny house.

Bringing the whirring drone of the sewing machine to a halt, Jasmine lifted her head to hear the sound of loud knocking, and she narrowed her eyes. Eyes which were tired and gritty from sewing until late last night. She rubbed them with the back of her fist, and yawned. Who was disturbing her during this quiet time when she'd got a rare opportunity to do some work? For a moment she was tempted to ignore it and stay there, neatly hemming the velvet curtains which needed to be delivered to her demanding client by next Wednesday, at the latest.

But she chided herself as she got up from her work spot in the corner of the sitting room and went to answer the unexpected summons. Surely she wasn't being suspicious just because someone was knocking at the door? If she wasn't careful she would become one of those sad people who became nervous at the thought of an unplanned caller. Who twitched whenever they heard a loud noise and were too scared to face the world outside. Just because she'd recently completed a radical lifestyle change and moved out of the city lock, stock and barrel didn't mean she had to start acting like some kind of hermit! Especially since she had discovered nothing but friendliness from the locals since arriving in this quiet hamlet—

a factor which had helped cushion her sudden and dramatic change in circumstances. It was probably somebody selling raffle tickets for the local spring fayre.

She pulled open the door.

It wasn't.

It most definitely wasn't.

Shock coursed through her like a tidal wave. She could feel the physical effects of it and fleetingly thought how much they resembled desire. The rapid increase in her pulse and the rush of blood to her face. The wobbly knees, which made her glad she was gripping the door handle for support. And most of all, that slightly out-of-body sensation, which made her think this couldn't be happening.

It couldn't.

Heart still pounding, she studied the man who was standing on her doorstep—as if he might disappear in a puff of smoke if she stared at him long enough. But he stayed exactly where he was, as solid as dark marble and as vital as the mighty oak tree which towered over the nearby village green. She wanted to somehow be immune to him but how could she, when just seeing him again made her heart clench with longing and her body quiver with long-suppressed lust?

His face was angled—slashed with hard planes and contours which spoke of an aristocratic lineage, even if his proud bearing hadn't confirmed it. With hair as black as coal and eyes a gleaming shade almost as dark, his rich gold complexion was dominated by a hawk-like nose and the most sensual lips she'd ever seen. Yet the suit he wore contradicted his identity for it was urbane and modern, as was the crisp white shirt and silken tie. But Jasmine had seen photos of him in flowing robes, which made him look as if he'd stepped straight from the pages of a fairy tale. Pale robes which had emphasised his burnished skin and hinted at a hard body which had been honed on the saddle of a horse, in one of the world's most unforgiving desert landscapes.

Zuhal Al Haidar—sheikh and royal prince. Second son of an ancient dynasty which ruled the oil-rich country of Razrastan, where diamonds had been discovered close to its immense mountains and world-class racing horses were bred. The man to whom she had given her body and heart—although he had wanted only her body and she had pretended to be okay with that because there hadn't been an alternative. Well, the alternative would have been to have spurned his unexpected advances and that had been something she'd found herself unable to do. There hadn't been a day since they'd parted that she hadn't thought about him but she'd never thought she'd see him again because he had cut her out of his life completely.

And that was the thing she needed to remember. That he hadn't wanted her. He'd cast her aside like yesterday's newspaper. She bit her lip as questions flooded through her mind.

Why was he here?

And then, much more crucial…

She mustn't let him stay here.

But Jasmine wasn't stupid. At least, not any more. She might once have acted like a complete idiot where Zuhal was concerned, but not now. She had grown up since splitting with him. She'd had to. She'd learned that you sometimes had to stop and think about what was the best thing to do in the long term, rather than what you really wanted to do. So she resisted the urge to close the door firmly in his face and instead forced a polite smile to her lips.

'Good heavens, Zuhal,' she said, in a voice which sounded strangely calm. 'This is a... surprise.'

Zuhal frowned, irritation dwarfing the anticipation which was shafting through him. It wasn't the greeting he had been expecting. Surely she should have been rapturously hurling herself into his arms by now? Even if she had decided to act out a little game-playing resistance for the sake of her pride, he still would have expected to see her eyes darkening with desire, or the parting of those rosy lips in unconscious invitation.

But no. Instead of desire he saw wariness and something else. Something he didn't recognise. Just as he didn't recognise the woman who stood before him. He remembered Jazz Jones as being a bit of a fashion queen. Someone who was always beautifully turned out— even if she'd made most of her clothes herself because her budget had been tight. But she had always had a definite *style* about her—it had been one of the things which had first drawn him to her, and presumably why the Granchester Hotel had employed her as manager in its sleek London boutique.

He remembered her honey-coloured hair

swinging to her chin, not grown out and tied back into a functional plait, which hung down the back of a plain jumper, which inexplicably had some unidentifiable stain on the shoulder. Her legs weren't on show either; their shapely curves were covered by a pair of very ugly jeans—a garment she'd never worn in his company after he'd explained his intense dislike of them.

But he told himself that her clothes didn't matter, because he didn't intend her to be wearing them for much longer. Nothing mattered—other than the yearning which was already heating his blood like a fever. And wasn't it ironic that Zuhal found himself resenting this sensual power she'd always had over him, even while his body hungrily responded to it? He let his voice dip into a velvety caress as it had done so often in the past, adopting the intimate tone of two people who had once been lovers. *And who would soon be lovers again.* 'Hello, Jazz.'

But there was no lessening of her wary expression. No answering smile or impulsive opening of the door to admit him to her home and her arms. No ecstatic acknowledgement that he was here, after nearly two years of not seeing each other. Instead, she nodded in recognition and once again there was a flash of something he didn't recognise in her eyes.

'How did you find me?'

He raised his eyebrows, because her unwelcoming attitude was something he wasn't familiar with—and neither was her bald question, which was bordering on the insolent. Was she really planning to interrogate him as if he were a passing salesman? Did she think it acceptable to leave the future King of Razrastan standing on her doorstep?

His words became tinged with a distinct note of reprimand, which had been known to make grown men shudder. 'Isn't this a conversation we should be having in the comfort of your home, Jazz, even if it doesn't strike me as very *comfortable*?'

She flinched. She actually flinched—before seeming to pull herself together. She was smiling now, but he could sense it was forced, as if she were pushing her mouth against the soft resistance of slowly setting concrete. He was confused. Hadn't they parted on good terms— or as good as they could be when a man was terminating what had been a very satisfying relationship? Although Jazz had been that little bit different from his other lovers, he recalled. She alone had refused to accept the keepsake piece of jewellery he always offered his ex-lovers as a memento. To his surprise—and, yes, his annoyance too—she had carefully repackaged the emerald and diamond pendant, along with a polite note telling him she couldn't possibly accept such a generous gift.

His mouth hardened as he looked at the peeling paint on the front door. She above all people could have done with an injection of cash.

'I'm afraid you can't come in,' she was saying. 'I'm sorry, Zuhal. It isn't…well, it isn't really convenient right now. Perhaps if you'd given me some warning.'

And then he understood. Of course. It was exactly as he had anticipated. Outwardly, she had accepted their break-up with dignity and a remarkable absence of begging, or tantrums. As he recalled, she hadn't even shed a single tear when he'd ended their affair—at least, not in his presence. But Jasmine Jones wasn't made of stone. She was the sexiest woman he'd ever met and had thrived under his expert tuition. Having awoken her body, surely he wouldn't have expected her to return to her celibate lifestyle after he'd introduced her to the joys of sex?

He felt the slow and heavy beat of a pulse to his temple. It was hard to believe—but why wouldn't she have replaced him in her bed with someone more suitable? Someone of her own class who might be willing or able to marry her. Perhaps he should have rung first. Or written. Given her time to prepare herself—to rid herself of her current squeeze and pretty herself up for his arrival. But since when did Zuhal Al Haidar ever have to ring ahead to make some sort of appointment?

He attempted to sound reasonable but could do nothing about the sudden dark clench of jealousy in his gut. 'You have another man in your life, Jazz?'

She looked genuinely taken aback—as if he had said something shocking and contemptible. 'Of course not!'

Zuhal expelled a breath he hadn't even realised he was holding. And wasn't it crazy how swiftly jealousy could become an overwhelming sense of triumph and then hot anticipation? 'Well, then. I have come a long way to see you.' He smiled. 'As I recall, when we went our separate ways we did it in the most civilised way possible. Which makes me wonder why you are so reluctant to let me in. Isn't that the modern way, for lovers to remain friends? To sit and talk of old times, with affection.'

Jasmine felt her body stiffen, grateful her left hand was still hidden behind the partially open door. Glancing over the Sheikh's burly shoulder, she could see the black gleam of his limousine sitting in the narrow lane, easily visible through the still-bare bushes. She supposed his driver was sitting there waiting, as people always waited for Zuhal. His bodyguards would be there, too, and there would probably be another carload of security people a little further along the lane, hidden from sight.

Hidden from sight.

Her heart contracted painfully but she tried to keep her face serene, even though the fear inside her was growing. She'd been so certain that the course she had taken had been the right one but now, as she looked into the carved perfection of Zuhal's dark features, she felt the disconcerting flurry of doubt—along with the far more worrying pang of recognition. What should she do?

If she refused to let him in it would arouse his suspicions—she knew it would. It would arouse his interest too, because he was alpha enough to always want what was denied him. And she still had at least an hour of freedom before the matter became more urgent than academic. So why not ask him inside? Find out what he had come for and politely listen before sending him on his way, no harm done. She felt the prick of conscience as she opened the door wider and saw him register the gold ring she wore on her wedding finger, and she saw his face darken as he bent his head to accommodate the low ceiling.

'I thought you said there wasn't a man in your life,' he accused as the door swung squeakily shut behind him.

'There isn't.'

'So why the wedding ring?' he demanded. 'Are you back with your husband?'

She flushed. 'Of course I'm not. That was never going to happen. We're divorced, Zuhal. You knew that. I was divorced when I met you.'

'So why the ring?' he demanded again.

Jasmine told herself he had no right to ask her questions about her personal life and maybe she should tell him so—but that would be pointless because Zuhal had never been brought up to conform to the rules of normal behaviour. And wasn't the truth that he *did* have the right to ask, even if he was unaware of it? She felt another painful twist of conscience before realising he was appraising her with a look she recognised only too well. The look which said he was hungry for her body. And that was all he ever wanted you for, she reminded herself bitterly. When the chips were down he wasn't offering you any kind of future. He took without giving anything back and she needed to protect herself to make sure that never happened again.

He was probably married by now—married to the suitable royal bride he had always told her he would one day marry.

She needed to get rid of him.

'I wear the ring as a deterrent,' she said.

He raised his dark eyebrows. 'Because men are regularly beating down your door with lustful intention?'

Ignoring the sardonic tone of his query, she shook her head. 'Hardly.'

'It's true that your appearance is a little

drab,' he conceded. 'But we both know how magnificent you can look when you try.'

Jasmine gritted her teeth, telling herself not to rise to the backhanded compliment. 'I realised I hadn't made the best relationship choices in the past and that I needed some time on my own,' she explained. 'Time to get my career up and running.'

'And what career might that be, Jazz?' he questioned softly. 'What made you stop working at the hotel boutique—I thought it paid reasonably well?'

Jasmine shrugged. She wasn't going to tell him about her soft furnishings business, which was still in an embryo stage but gaining in popularity all the time. Or her plans for designing baby clothes, which she hoped would one day provide her with a modest living. Because none of that was any of his business. 'London was getting too expensive and I wanted a change,' she said. 'And you still haven't told me why you're here.'

With genuine surprise, Zuhal realised that maybe he had misjudged his impact on her. Was it possible she hadn't been as besotted by him as he'd thought—and that she wouldn't take him into her bed without forethought or ceremony, as she'd done so often in the past? He remembered how her soft and undemanding nature had always acted like a balm on his troubled senses. How she had always been eager and hungry to see him. But now her distinct lack of interest punctured his erotic thoughts and instead he was filled with the unusual urge to confide in her. He sighed as he walked to the window and looked out at the yellow flash of the few straggly daffodils which were poking out from the overgrown grass in the tiny garden.

'You know my brother is missing?' he questioned, without preamble. 'Presumed dead.'

She gasped and when he turned round her fingers were lying against her throat, as if she were starved of air. '*Dead?*' she managed eventually. 'No, I didn't know that. Oh, Zuhal, I'm so sorry. I mean, I never met him—obviously—but I remember he was your only sibling.'

He narrowed his eyes. 'We kept it quiet for as long as possible, but now it's out there in the public domain. You hadn't heard?'

She shook her head. 'I don't… I don't get much chance to read the papers these days. World news is so depressing—and my TV isn't actually working at the moment,' she added, before biting down on the lushness of her lower lip and fixing him with a wary look. 'What happened, or would you rather not talk about it?'

He'd thought she might take him in her arms and comfort him and wasn't that what he wanted more than anything else? To feel the warmth of another body—the soft squeeze of flesh reminding him that he was very much alive instead of lying prone and cold somewhere in a merciless desert, while vultures hovered overhead. But she didn't. She just stood on the other side of the small room, her green-gold eyes dark with distress, though her body language remained stiff and awkward—as if she didn't know how to be around him.

But still he found himself talking about it, in a way he might not have done so freely with anyone else. Almost imperceptibly, his voice grew harsh. 'Although Kamal was King of Razrastan, with all the responsibilities which came with that exalted role, my brother never lost his love of recklessness.'

'I do remember you saying he was a bit of a daredevil,' she offered cautiously.

He gave another heavy sigh as he nodded. 'He was. All through his youth he embraced the most dangerous of sports and nobody could do a thing to stop him. Our father tried often enough, but our mother actively encouraged his daring behaviour. Which was why he piloted his own plane and heli-skied whenever possible. Why he deep-sea-dived and climbed the world's most challenging mountains—and nobody could deny that he excelled at everything he put his mind to.' He paused. 'His coronation as King inevitably curtailed most of these activities, but he was still prone to taking off on his horse, often alone. He said it gave him time to think. To be away from the hurly-burly of palace life. And that's what happened last year...'

'What did?' she prompted uneasily as his words tailed off.

Zuhal felt the inevitable sense of sorrow mounting inside him but there was bitterness, too. Because hadn't Kamal's actions impacted on so many people—and on him more than anyone? 'One morning he mounted his beloved Akhal-Teke horse and rode off into the desert as the sun was rising, or so one of the stable boys told us later. By the time we realised he had ridden off unaccompanied, a fierce storm was blasting its way through the desert. Even from within the protection of the palace walls we could see the sky growing as red as blood and the wind whipping itself up into a wild frenzy.'

His voice grew unsteady for a moment before he continued. 'They say there is no escape from the blanket of sand which results from those storms, that it infiltrates everything. You can't see, or hear, or breathe. For a while it feels as if hell has unleashed all its demons and set them free upon the world.' He swallowed. 'We never found either of them— neither man nor horse—during one of the biggest search operations our country has ever mounted. Not a trace. It is inconceivable that he could have survived such an onslaught.' There was a pause as his mouth twisted. 'And the desert is very efficient at disposing of bodies.'

'Oh, Zuhal,' she whispered. 'That's awful. I'm so sorry for your loss.'

He gave a brief nod of his head, dismissing her soft words of sympathy because he hadn't come here for *words*. 'We're all sorry,' he said matter-of-factly.

'So what will happen?'

'Kamal cannot be officially pronounced

dead for seven years, but the law states that the country cannot be without a king during that time.' Like a boxer in the ring, Zuhal clenched his fists so that the knuckles cracked and turned deathly white beneath the olive skin. 'And so, I have agreed to rule in his absence.'

She blinked at him as if the significance of what he had told her had only just sunk in. 'What exactly does that…mean?'

'It means that in seven years' time, if Kamal has still not returned, then I will be crowned, since I am the sole surviving heir. Until that time I will be King in everything but name, and I will be known as the Sheikh Regent.'

It was the mention of the word *heir* which set Jasmine's senses jangling with renewed fear. A trickle of sweat whispered down her back and settled at the base of her spine, soaking into the waistband of her jeans. Did he *know*? Was that why he was here today?

But no, of course he didn't know. He wouldn't be standing there with that bleak look on his face talking about his powerful new role if he had any inkling of the momentous thing which had happened in *her* life. And there were reasons he didn't know, she reminded herself painfully. Reasons which had helped spur her desire to stop reading the papers and listening to the news.

'And is your *wife*...' Somehow her voice didn't tremble on the word. 'Is she happy about her position as the new ruler's consort?'

'My wife?' he echoed, frowning at her uncomprehendingly. 'I don't have a wife, Jazz.'

'But I thought...' Jasmine swallowed as her perceived view of the world did a dramatic shift. 'I thought you were seeing a princess from a neighbouring desert region, soon after we split. Zara, I think her name was.'

Zuhal nodded. 'I was.' His eyes narrowed as they swept over her. 'Yes, Zara was the latest in a long line of mooted royal brides, with a pedigree almost equal to my own.' He shrugged. 'But she had a laugh which used to set my teeth on edge and I could not contemplate a life-long partnership with her. And back then, there was no sense of urgency. Now it is different, of course. Now I must rule my country and for that I will need a wife by my side.'

Jasmine's heart flooded with heat and began to pound loudly with something which felt like hope, even though afterwards she would ask herself how she could have been so stupid. But for a few seconds she actually allowed herself to believe in the fantasy which still haunted her some nights when sleep stubbornly refused to come—of her desert prince returning to sweep her off her feet. 'I still don't understand,' she said cautiously, 'why you're here.'

He lifted up the palms of his hands like a man on the point of surrender. 'I'll tell you exactly why I'm here, Jazz,' he said, a hard smile flattening the edges of his sensual lips. 'Next month my life will change beyond recognition, when I sign the papers which are currently being drawn up to officially recognise me as the Sheikh Regent. But beneath all the inevitable celebrations that the line will continue my people are grieving and uncertain, for my brother's disappearance has unsettled them. The country needs stability and they are looking to me to provide it, for while Kamal had many commendable character traits, steadfastness was not one of them. I need a bride,' he said, not seeming to notice that she had gasped again, or that her hands had started trembling. 'But this time I cannot afford to be picky. I must marry someone suitable—and quickly.'

She gulped the words out breathlessly. She just couldn't help herself. 'Someone l-like?'

'Someone of royal blood. Obviously.' His black eyes crinkled with that rare flash of mischief which used to tie her up in knots. 'Not a divorced girl from England, I'm afraid, Jazz— just in case you were getting your hopes up.'

'I wasn't,' she said, furious with him, but even more furious with herself—for allowing herself that stupid little daydream which had made her heart begin to race. Hadn't she learnt *anything* during the time she'd been his secret mistress? That she was as disposable as an empty baked-beans can? 'Is that why you're here, Zuhal?' she demanded. 'To talk about your marriage prospects? What were you hoping for—my advice? Perhaps you'd like me to help you vet your future bride for you?'

'No, that's not why I'm here. Do you want me to show you why I'm here, my beautiful Jazz?' He had started moving across the small room until he was standing right in front of her. Until he had pulled her without warning into his powerful arms, his black eyes glittering with pain and desire and something else, as he stared down into her face. 'I'm here because I'm empty and aching and because I know you can take that ache away.'

She should have given him a piece of her mind. Should have told him she wasn't just something he could put down and then pick up again, as the whim took him. So why didn't she? Was it his touch which made common sense fly out of the window, or just the yearning inside her which had never gone away? She should have realised that by *aching* he meant sex, but for one crazy moment Jasmine thought he was talking about his heart. So she let him tilt her chin with those strong, olive-dark fingers, just as she let his mouth travel towards hers in what felt like a slow extension of time. She had to urge herself not to rise up on tiptoe to make the kiss come sooner, but somehow she retained enough restraint to hold back. But perhaps that wasn't such a good idea because by the time their lips touched, she felt a flash of connection so intense that she gave a little moan of joy.

And Jazz forgot everything. Forgot why he shouldn't be there and why she shouldn't be reacting to him like this. Why it was wrong to allow his strong hands to burrow beneath the thick-knit sweater she was wearing and to cup her breasts with luxuriant familiarity. It felt like the best place she'd been for a very long time as his mouth explored hers with a thoroughness which left her reeling, his tongue licking at her with intimate familiarity. The blood pumped through her veins like honey as she felt the drift of his fingers over her nipples—briefly flicking over the engorged buds before creeping down to her torso.

And this was heaven. Jasmine's throat dried as he reacquainted himself with the curve of her belly and she wriggled accommodatingly as he slipped his thumb beneath the waistband of her jeans and began to tease the warm, bare skin. Did she suck her stomach in, hoping that he would move his hands further inside the thick denim to caress her where she was hot and wet and longing to be caressed, and didn't she want that more than anything else? She could feel the hard press of his erection and instinctively her thighs parted by a fraction and she could hear his low murmur of appreciation.

He drew his lips away. 'You've changed shape,' he observed unevenly.

'Y-yes.' She nearly asked him whether or not he liked it—and how crazy was *that*?—

when a sudden thought hit her like a squirt of icy water and fear began to whisper over her. Drawing in a deep breath, she looked directly into his eyes as comprehension began to dawn on her. 'Are you here just because...because you want to have sex with me, Zuhal?'

He seemed momentarily taken aback by her question but she knew the moment she saw him shrug that her worst fear was true. Well, maybe not her *worst* fear...

'You...you want some kind of physical release, is that it?' she continued unsteadily. 'Some easy, uncomplicated sex, before you return home in search of your suitable royal bride?'

At least he had the grace to look abashed but the look was quickly replaced by one of defiance. 'What did you expect, Jazz?' he murmured. 'That I would present to my very conservative people a foreign divorcee as the woman I had chosen?' His black gaze burned into her. 'We both know that was always going to be a non-starter. Just as we both know that the chemistry which has always sparked between us is still there. Nothing about that has changed. I still want you so much that I could explode with it—and so do you. You come alive whenever I touch you, don't you? Your body cries out for mine, the same way it always did. So why waste it?' His voice dipped into a sensual caress. 'Why not give into what we both want—and make love one last and beautiful time?'

Dazedly, Jasmine listened to his arrogant statement—and didn't his attitude justify some of the tough decisions she'd been forced to make? She was about to tell him that it was a mistake to call what he had in mind *making love* and wondering if he would attempt to persuade her otherwise, when a distant sound changed everything. She moved away from him—not so quickly as to arouse suspicion—praying that Darius was only whimpering in some kind of happy little infant dream and would shortly go back to sleep.

But her prayers went unanswered. The whimper became louder. It morphed into a cry and then a protesting yell and she saw Zuhal's face change. Watched the black eyes narrow as his gaze swept questioningly over her and she quickly stared down at the threadbare rug for fear that he might see the sudden tears welling up in her eyes. She thought about all the things she *could* say.

She could pretend that it was a peacock, because weren't they supposed to sound like young babies? Or maybe that was babies younger than Darius which sounded like those squawking birds. And anyway, peacocks lived in the grounds of stately homes, didn't they? They promenaded elegantly over manicured lawns—their magnificent blue-green plumage wouldn't dream of gracing the scruffy little garden of a rented cottage just outside Oxford.

'What was that, Jazz?' Zuhal questioned ominously.

She knew then that the game was up. That she could attempt evasion to try to deflect his attention and send him on his way by pretending that the baby belonged to someone else and she was just childminding. But she couldn't. Not really—and not just because the time frame would prove her a liar. No. No matter what had happened in the past or how little Zuhal thought of her now, she was going to have to come clean. And hadn't she always wanted that anyway, on some subliminal level?

'What was that, Jazz?' he repeated, only now a note of something dangerous had been added into the mix to make his voice grow even darker.

Slowly she lifted her gaze to meet the accusation in his eyes and prepared for her whole world to change in the telling of a single sentence. 'It's my child. Or rather, our child,' she said, sucking in a breath of air. 'You have a son, Zuhal, and his name is Darius.'

CHAPTER TWO

AND THEN, AS IF by magic, Darius went back to sleep. Jasmine could hear it quite plainly in the sounds which were issuing from his baby monitor. The lessening of his cry into a gulping sob which gradually became a little coo, which was so much a feature of his daily nap. She knew he would now be peacefully asleep again and that if only her son's timing had been a little better, Zuhal would have been none the wiser.

But Jasmine knew there was no point wishing that Darius had delayed his cry until the Sheikh had been hurried away from the premises. If Zuhal hadn't been kissing her, then he would already have left. If she hadn't been stupidly *letting* him kiss her and wanting the kind of things she should be ashamed of wanting...

And anyway—wasn't this what she had always wanted to happen? Had tried to make happen, if she hadn't been blocked along the way by his position and power. *So don't let guilt beat you up*, she told herself fiercely, even though it was difficult not to flinch as she met the naked accusation in his black eyes. You've tried to do your best.

'My son?' he repeated incredulously.

She nodded. 'Yes, he—'

'Don't you dare say another word. Just take me to see him,' he cut over her words, his voice laced with a layer of ice she'd heard him use before—though never with her.

'You will see him. I promise—just not yet. Let him sleep, Zuhal. Please,' she said, with the confidence of someone who'd been bringing up a baby on her own for the last nine months and knew how cranky they could get if they were woken prematurely.

'I won't waken him but I want to see him.' His autocratic command hissed through the air. 'Take me to him, Jazz. Now.'

Her lips dry, Jasmine nodded. How had she ever thought she could oppose his wishes? She'd never managed it in the past—so why should now be any different? He had dumped her without warning—and, even though he had told her from the start that she could never have any future with him, it had still seemed to come out of the blue. But she had held it together then, just as she must hold it together now. 'Come with me,' she said in a low voice, the hairs on the back of her neck prickling with unease as she led the way from the room.

Feeling like a participant in some bizarre dream, Zuhal followed Jazz up the narrow staircase, his mind spinning with disbelief as she reached the top and gestured towards the open door of a nursery painted in sunny shades of yellow. He wanted to convince himself that she'd been lying and that it was no child of his who lay sleeping in a cot beneath the window. But as he silently crossed the room to gaze down at the infant, he knew there was absolutely no question that this was his baby. It was more than the shock of ebony hair so like his own. More than the olive skin, which was a paler version of his. It was something fundamental and almost *primitive* which activated a powerful surge of recognition deep within him as he gazed down at the gently parted lips of the baby boy. He saw Jazz tense as he reached down and briefly laid his forefinger against the baby's soft cheek, before withdrawing it and turning abruptly on his heel, to walk out the way he had come. He didn't say a word until they were back downstairs—he didn't trust himself to speak—and even though he wanted to rage and rail at her, he kept his voice low.

'Do you realise the constitutional significance of what you've done?' he hissed.

Jasmine flinched and a part of her wished she could have given into the luxury of tears if she hadn't recognised the need to stay strong. *Constitutional significance?* Was that the only thing he cared about in the light of his discovery? Of course it was. It was why he'd ended their relationship and why he had turned up here today, to use her body as he might use a stone vessel filled with water to quench his thirst. For him nothing mattered other than the needs and demands of his beloved country and everything else came second to that.

'Did you not think to tell me, Jazz?' he continued, still in that icy undertone of suppressed fury. 'That the seed of my loins had borne fruit?'

Jasmine shivered as his words created a powerful image in her mind which made her heart clench with impotent longing until she forced herself to push it away and focus on what was important. 'I did try to tell you.'

His cold expression suggested he didn't believe her. 'When?'

'After we…split up.' *When he'd sweetly informed her that she was the kind of woman who made a perfect mistress, but not the kind of woman he could ever marry.* 'Not for many weeks, it's true. I… I didn't realise I was pregnant. At least, not straight away.'

'Why not?' he bit out witheringly. 'You may have been a virgin when we met but please don't make out you were born yesterday, Jazz. What do you mean, you *didn't realise* you were pregnant? What, were you waiting for the stork to fly in through the window and surprise you?'

His words were cruel. Sarcastic. Deliberately so, it seemed. Jasmine tried to convince herself that his anger was understandable. Wouldn't she have felt just as angry if the situation were reversed—to have discovered that she'd become a parent and have been kept in the dark about it? 'I was all over the place,' she admitted. 'I was operating in a bit of a fog—on autopilot, if you like. Just getting through the day took all my energy and I felt disorientated because…well, it was *weird* getting used to life without you.'

Zuhal's lips tightened but to his surprise he found he couldn't disagree with her because he too had been disconcerted by the discovery that Jazz had left a peculiar hole in his life. He had explained it away by reminding himself that it had all been about sex—the best sex he'd ever had. Against all the odds she had captivated him—for he had never been with someone as low-born as her before. She'd been working in the boutique attached to London's famous Granchester Hotel where he'd been staying, and on a primitive level he had initially been drawn to her pert breasts and curvy hips. By the buttery swing of her blonde hair and the way her lips curved into a sweet smile whenever she was serving customers. But although many women caught his eye and made it clear they were his for the taking, Zuhal rarely gave into his most base desires. Sometimes he took pleasure in denying himself sexual gratification because deprivation was good for the spirit and what was easily gained was easily discarded. Plus, he liked a challenge—and a challenge had certainly been presented to him when the humble shop girl had blushed as he'd spoken to her and had had difficulty meeting his gaze.

His hunger ignited, he had been pleased to discover she was divorced because divorced women were often cynical about marriage, with few of the marital ambitions of single women, which bored the hell out of him. They also possessed an earthy expertise which made them the best lovers.

But Jazz hadn't been experienced.

He remembered his shock—and then his pleasure—when he had discovered her innocence. When she had opened those soft thighs and he had broken through the tight hymen, which had flagged up the gratifying knowledge that he was her first ever lover. He remembered the orgasm which had followed. Which had rocked him to the core of his being. And the one after, and the one after that...

With an effort he dragged his mind back to the present because none of that was relevant now. Not in the light of his discovery that she was a secretive little manipulator.

'Talk me through what happened, Jazz,' he bit out and could see her trying to compose herself, rubbing her hands up and down over the arms of her sweater, as if she were cold.

She swallowed. 'When you went back to Razrastan I just carried on as normal, terrified someone at the hotel was going to discover I'd been having intimate relations with a guest.'

'But nobody did?' he probed.

Jasmine shook her head. 'No. Not a soul. But then, we were very discreet, weren't we, Zuhal? You made sure of that. I was never even permitted to stay with you in your fancy penthouse suite and we only ever went to the borrowed house of one of your rich friends, under cover of darkness.'

'I have always tried to be discreet about my relationships—and the newspapers would have had a field day if they'd discovered I was sleeping with someone like you,' he said coldly.

'Someone like me?' she echoed.

'You know what I'm talking about. It was almost a cliché—the prince and the shop girl. In a way, I was protecting you.'

Jasmine bit her lip, because it had been much more likely he had been protecting his own precious reputation. Should she tell him how difficult it had felt to carry on serving behind the till with that bright smile pinned to her lips, when she had been missing him so much? Maybe it was the effort of that—of trying to appear normal—which had meant her first missed period had passed by without her noticing. And then when she *had* noticed something was amiss, she'd been unable to confide in anyone. Her parents were dead and she hadn't dared place her trust in friends and colleagues, terrified someone might run to the press with the story. She had a cousin she was close to, but Emily lived miles away and Jasmine had never felt quite so lonely.

Even now, as she looked up into Zuhal's flinty features, she could still remember the scary sense of isolation she'd felt as she'd realised she was pretty much on her own, with a tiny life to support. Factor in the fact that she'd been missing him so badly and you ended up with someone who had found herself in a precarious situation. 'I tried to ring you but your number came up as unobtainable.'

He met the question in her eyes. 'I make a point of regularly changing my phone number,' he informed her coolly. 'My security people tell me it's safer that way.'

'And, of course, it keeps troublesome ex-girlfriends at bay?' she guessed, forcing herself to confront the bitter truth.

He shrugged. 'Something like that,' he conceded. 'When did you try to contact me?'

Accurately, she was able to relay the exact month—because at that stage her pregnancy had been well established. She'd been determined to show Zuhal that she intended going ahead with the birth, with or without his approval. That she didn't need a man—or a husband—in order to survive, because experience had taught her that marriage was by no means the magic bullet which so many women imagined it was.

Feeling on firmer footing now, she sucked in a steadying breath. 'Eventually, I managed to get through to one of your aides. Adham, I think his name was. I told him I needed to speak to you urgently and he promised he would pass on the message to you.'

'But I never got it,' he said, his voice hardening.

'So blame him.'

'Adham is a loyal servant who would have been acting in my best interests. The palace was in uproar because of my brother's disappearance and, of course, that impacted profoundly on my future. And not just that.' His black eyes bored into her. 'Do you have any idea of the amount of women who are eager to speak to me, who try to phone the palace switchboard?'

'Strangely enough no, I don't,' she answered, colour rising in her cheeks so that suddenly she felt hot and uncomfortable. 'Tallying up the numbers of your ex-lovers isn't a pastime which has ever appealed to me.'

'You could have told him you were pregnant!' he accused. 'You knew that would have ensured you got through to me straight away. Why didn't you do that, Jazz?'

Jasmine licked her lips. Because she'd been scared. Scared of Zuhal's influence and of the reality of confronting it for the first time. He'd always left his sheikh status at the door of the bedroom, but during that brief and fruitless phone call, she'd got an inkling of the real man behind the very sexy facade. It had taken her ages to get through to his office and during the long wait she'd realised just how powerful her former lover really was. She remembered the way his aide had spoken to her—as if she were a piece of dirt he'd found on the bottom of his shoe. And she'd been fearful that, although Zuhal obviously didn't want her any more, he might want to claim sole custody of their baby—and he'd have the wherewithal to make it happen.

And that was something she could never allow.

'You told me you were planning to marry a royal princess,' she reminded him. 'I thought that was another reason why your aide was so *off* with me. There were reports about your burgeoning romance in all the papers. About how two desert kingdoms were going to be united and it was going to be the greatest thing to happen in the region for decades. The Dream Desert ticket, I think the tabloids called it.' Which had been another reason why she'd stopped reading them. 'Wouldn't it have completely ruined everything if some casual lover had come forward with the news that you were to become a father?'

Zuhal's eyes narrowed as he forced himself to dismiss her persuasive words. Because weren't these accusations and counter-accusations diverting his attention from the monumental discovery he had just made?

He had a son.

A ready-made heir.

Perhaps fate was showing him a little benevolence for once.

He looked at the woman standing in front of him. A few minutes ago he'd been kissing her and her response had indicated that if it hadn't been for the baby's cry, she would have allowed him to be deep inside her by now. *Would* she, he found himself wondering, with a brand-new disdain which had blossomed as a result of his unbelievable discovery? Had she become one of those women who would cast aside the needs of her baby in pursuit of her own carnal pleasures? And if that were the case, then wouldn't that be easy to prove in a court of law—thereby putting him in a morally superior position and demonstrating his own suitability to bring up the child, instead of her? Surely that would be simpler all round.

He noted the trepidation flickering in the depths of her green-gold eyes as she returned his gaze, just as he noted the sudden tension which was stiffening her narrow shoulders. The silence between them was growing into something immense and uncomfortable but, unlike most people would be, Zuhal was unperturbed by it. Indeed, he often *orchestrated* silence when necessary, for it was a powerful tool in negotiation and never had negotiation been more vital than now.

'How are you managing for money?' he questioned casually.

He could see a look of faint confusion criss-cross her brow and wondered if she was dis-orientated by his sudden change of subject.

'I manage,' she said defensively.

'I said "how", Jazz?'

She shrugged. 'I sew.'

He frowned. 'You sew?'

'Yes. You remember. I always liked sewing. I was planning to go to fashion college when my mother got sick and I had to defer my place to look after her.'

He thought back. Had she told him that? Even if she *had*, he suspected it would have gone in one ear and straight out of the other. He hadn't really been interested in her past, just as he hadn't been interested in her future, because he'd known there could never be one—not for them. The only thing which had interested him, and for a time had obsessed him, had been the magnificence of her body and the sheer sexual dynamite of their coming together.

'That's right,' he prevaricated as some long-buried fact swam up from the depths of his subconscious. 'You wanted to be a fashion de-signer. Is that what you're doing now?'

She gave him the kind of look which suggested he had no idea how normal mortals lived. 'I wish,' she said. 'You can't just set yourself up as a fashion designer, Zuhal, especially when you've got no real qualifications. For one thing, the overheads would be prohibitive, and for another, there's a whole heap of competition out there. You see that sewing machine over there?' Her finger trembled a little as she pointed to it. 'That's what I was doing when you arrived. Mostly, I specialise in soft furnishings—cushions and curtains, that sort of thing. People always need those and Oxford isn't far away. There are plenty of folk with deep pockets who change their decor all the time, even if there's nothing wrong with it. Probably because they're rich and bored and can't think of anything better to do,' she added.

She seemed eager to deflect his attention from the life-changing news with her mundane chatter, he thought grimly. And she would be, wouldn't she? But her words made him consider both her income and her environment and for the first time Zuhal took proper notice of his surroundings, his lips curving with ill-concealed contempt. The furniture was of the cheapest variety, the rug threadbare and the paint on the window frames peeling. Only the curtains and cushions redeemed the place, their brightness adding an unexpected touch of jollity to the small room. Presumably her own handiwork.

His disdain turned into anger. And she was bringing up his son in a place like this! The heir to the Al Haidar dynasty was growing up in some scruffy little house on the outskirts of Oxford, with no security at the door and barely enough warmth inside. He wanted to berate her. To tell her she was unfit to care for his child, but something made him bite back his words as he sensed that hostility would be counterproductive to his cause. He looked at her faded jeans and the sweater with that ugly stain on the shoulder. Wouldn't it be sensible to offer her an easy way out? To leave her free to live the kind of life she had been destined to live before their paths had unpredictably crossed in an upmarket London hotel.

'We need to discuss the future,' he said.

She looked at him warily. 'What do you mean?'

He took a step closer and then wished he hadn't because her unsophisticated soapy scent suddenly made his senses become keen and raw. And wasn't it crazy that, despite his anger, he could still feel the powerful jerk of his erection pressing uncomfortably hard against the zipper of his trousers? Hadn't she always had that power over him—and hadn't it been that power which had made him terminate their relationship sooner than he'd intended?

'What do you think I mean, Jazz?' he demanded. 'Did you think I would be content to be granted a brief look at my son before shrugging my shoulders and walking away? That I would be prepared to say goodbye to a child who has been kept a stranger to me until now?'

She swallowed. 'Of course I didn't.'

'You say that with remarkably little conviction!' he accused.

'Because it's all happened so quickly! I wasn't expecting you to just turn up like this, Zuhal. It's difficult to know what to think.'

'At least we are agreed on something,' he said. 'Though I think that, of the two of us, I have received by far the greater surprise today. I need a little time to assess the situation properly and work out where we must go from here. Decisions made in the heat of the moment will benefit no one, least of all my son.'

'You mean...' Her green-gold eyes looked hopeful. 'You mean you'll go back to Razrastan and contact me when you've had a chance to mull it over?'

He gave a short laugh. 'Go back to Razrastan? Are you really that naïve, Jazz? Do you think that, having found my child, I will now exit myself from his life?' Ruthlessly, he found himself taking pleasure from her lip-biting response to his words. And why *shouldn't* he enjoy her distress? She hadn't given *his* feelings a second thought when she'd kept his progeny hidden from him, had she? 'I will return later to take you to dinner. Somewhere neutral away from here, where we can consider our options. I will have one of my people book somewhere suitable.'

'No. I can't. That isn't going to work,' she protested. 'I'm not leaving Darius while I go out for dinner with you!'

'Why not?' he demanded. 'Do you think I'm going to have him spirited away while you're out?'

She met his gaze with a fierce challenge on her face—a look he had never seen her use before. 'I wouldn't put it past you.'

He inclined his head in unwilling admiration. 'You are wise indeed not to underestimate my determination,' he conceded. 'But you still haven't explained your refusal to dine with me.'

'Because I don't have a local babysitter, not yet,' she babbled. 'And I'm not leaving Darius with a stranger!'

His lips twisted. 'You think I would compromise childcare, Jazz? He is a royal Prince of Razrastan—and he will be cared for by the finest professional money can buy.'

'No.'

'*No?*' he verified incredulously.

'I'm not leaving him with a stranger,' she repeated stubbornly.

A pulse flickered at his temple as he trained his gaze on the minuscule kitchen which could just be glimpsed over her shoulder. 'You expect me to eat dinner here?'

'I don't particularly care whether you eat or not, since food is the last thing on my mind,' she returned. 'But since you are determined to have this meeting, I dare say I can rustle up something for supper.'

There was a moment of tense silence before, slowly, he nodded his head. 'Very well. I will return at eight.' He paused. 'In the meantime, my bodyguards will be stationed around the property, so if you're contemplating making some dramatic break for freedom, I urge you think again.'

Jasmine stared at him, feeling as if she was being backed into a corner. Was that how he intended her to feel? As if he had all the power and she had none? *Because that was true, wasn't it?* She looked at him. 'Bodyguards?' she echoed. 'Are you out of your mind? We've been living here perfectly safely for the last six months. This is rural Oxfordshire. We don't need bodyguards.'

'On the contrary, you most certainly do. You may have lived that way in the past, Jazz, but those days are over. This child has pure Al Haidar blood pulsing through his veins and will be treated accordingly.' He slanted her a warning look. 'I will see you later. Just make sure you are ready to receive me.'

His final request was like a throwback to the past and she wondered how she was supposed to do that. Was he hinting that he'd like her to be waiting for him wearing some tiny scrap of silk-satin lingerie the way she'd done in the past—showing as much flesh as possible without actually being naked? She studied his hard face. Unlikely. At this precise moment, his expression betrayed nothing but contempt. His bearing was both regal and imperious as he turned and walked out of the front door, closing it softly behind him. Jasmine could hear the purr of a powerful car engine as it started to move and now that the shock of seeing him again had begun to wear off, she began to tremble.

Unwanted tears stung her eyes, but she brushed them away as she tried to centre herself and make sense of what had just happened and to wonder how it had all come to this.

She heard Darius beginning to wake again and determination flooded through her in a hot rush as she recognised that she needed to have her wits about her when dealing with a man as powerful as Zuhal.

But most of all she needed to be strong.

CHAPTER THREE

SHE SHOULD NEVER have fallen for the royal Sheikh—that was the thought which plagued Jasmine for the rest of the afternoon, even while she was playing peep-oh with Darius then splashing him in the bath and making him giggle in that heartbreakingly innocent way of his.

But Zuhal had been determined to seduce her, despite the fact that she had been a shop girl and he a royal prince of noble descent. Her marriage had ended and she'd been feeling a failure when the Sheikh had waltzed into the Granchester boutique and subjected her to a highly effective charm offensive. She remembered his dark gaze licking over her skin and it had felt like being bathed in sweet black molasses. Sensing an unknown danger, she had let the other, rather pushy assistant deal with him, but her reluctance to engage had only seemed to increase his desire. Had she been surprised when he had turned up the following day to subject her to some more of that lazy charm? Not really. And she would have challenged any woman with a pulse to have resisted him for long. The strict rules of the hotel concerning relationships between guests and staff meant their resulting flirtation had been conducted amid great secrecy, and afterwards she'd realised that had probably added an extra layer of piquancy.

But the tumultuous ending of her marriage had left her feeling undesirable and Zuhal had changed all that so, of course, she'd agreed to have dinner with him. The restaurant had been small and badly lit—chosen mainly for discretion, she'd suspected—and even though the implied secrecy of that had been a little disappointing, already she'd been in too deep to care. To her astonishment—but not his—she had ended up in bed with him.

It had been…bliss. No other word for it. The soft plunder of his lips. His slow undressing as he had peeled off her cheap clothes. Her first sight of him naked—all that honed and burnished flesh and the unmistakable evidence of just how much he'd wanted her. She should have been shy, or even daunted—but she had been neither. In fact, she had been wet and ready, uttering nameless pleas as he'd stroked erotic pathways over her heated skin. Even the brief pain of losing her virginity hadn't marred her mounting enjoyment and Zuhal had confessed afterwards that it had added an extra layer of excitement to his. Orgasm had followed orgasm and he hadn't said anything until afterwards, when she'd been lying gazing up at the ceiling in dazed disbelief as he'd circled a puckered nipple with one careless finger. Turning her flushed face towards his, he had drawled out a single word.

'Why?'

And then she'd told him about Richard and her non-consummated marriage. About how he'd insisted on waiting until their wedding night and how flattered she had been by that seemingly old-fashioned restraint. Because she'd thought it was an essential ingredient for a happy marriage—though she had been basing her opinion on guesswork rather than experience, because she had no idea what a happy marriage was like. Because she'd blocked her eyes and ears to the reality of her own parents' marriage for so long, hadn't she? She'd learnt to ignore dark undercurrents and pretend they simply weren't happening. She'd become an expert in normalising dysfunctional relationships. As if by normalising them it would make everything all right…but of course, it never did. She had been the lonely child, caught in the crossfire of two warring parents. And it had been hell. Perhaps that had been another reason why she'd agreed to become Richard's wife. He had felt *safe*—a bit like a small boat discovering a calm harbour after a rocky and unpredictable voyage.

Yet when her own wedding night had come—sex just hadn't happened. It had been embarrassing and disappointing and as time had gone on and still she'd remained a virgin, Jasmine had asked Richard whether it was something to do with her. It was then that he had broken down in tears to tell her he actually preferred men. To be honest, it had come as something of a relief to know the simple cause of their incompatibility and Jasmine had wished him well before they had separated. But it had left her wondering whether she was a bad judge of character not to have picked up on it before.

She had also wondered if Zuhal would think

her less of a woman because of her unusual past. Or if her lack of experience would turn him off, but, to her pleasure and surprise, it had seemed to do the exact opposite.

'Perfect,' he'd murmured, while fingering her quivering flesh. 'Just perfect.'

'Wh-what is?' she remembered asking dazedly.

And that was when he'd explained that being a divorcee automatically precluded her from any kind of future with him, just in case she'd been getting any ideas—something she'd denied vehemently.

But afterwards she'd wondered just how true her denial had been. She'd told him she never expected anything from their relationship other than pleasure, so how did that explain the river of tears she'd cried when they'd made love for the very last time?

She needed to remember that. Every bit of it. To remind herself of just how ruthless Zuhal could be—and just how stupidly sensitive *she* could be. He had all the wealth and the power while she had none, but she had something far more precious: her gorgeous little black-haired baby who was the light of her life. She wasn't going to be unreasonable—just as long as Zuhal wasn't. He needed to understand that, despite the huge differences between them, in their roles as parents they would be equals.

She laid Darius down in his crib and went through the lullaby routine she'd begun after bringing him home from the hospital. She remembered how scared she'd been, yet determined to love her little baby with all her heart. But Darius had been easy to love. An easy baby all round. He hadn't cried incessantly at night, nor been difficult to feed. Had he somehow sensed that Jasmine had been having a tough time adapting to life as a single mum and, in some loyal baby way, had made it as simple as possible for her?

Her hair was still damp from bath-time play and she certainly hadn't got around to changing her clothes when Jasmine heard an authoritative rap on the door. But she wasn't planning on trying to make herself look presentable to Zuhal, was she? To slip into something glamorous so he might look at her with admiration rather than contempt. Apart from the fact that it was so long since she had dressed up for a night out, mightn't that send out the wrong message? Zuhal had one role to play in her life and that was as a father. She bit her lip.

Which meant she needed to put all thoughts of the other stuff out of her mind. The kisses and the caresses and the scarily fast way he could always make her come. The way she'd almost succumbed in his arms earlier...

Even so, she couldn't quite block out her foreboding as she ran downstairs, because she suspected that remaining immune to Zuhal was going to be easier said than done. Heart racing, she pulled open the door to greet him, wishing his impact weren't always so over-whelming. But it was. Every time she saw him she felt as if someone had squeezed her heart within an iron fist and wouldn't let it go. Unlike her, Zuhal *had* changed his clothes— adopting the casual attire which occasionally permitted him to go as incognito as was pos-sible when you were the possessor of such head-turning good looks. His soft black jacket meant he smelt faintly of leather, underpinned with that subtle scent of sandalwood which was so much a part of him. Dark jeans hugged the powerful length of his thighs and his jaw was shadowed with the new growth which ap-peared so soon after he'd shaved, reminding her of just how virile he'd always seemed to her innocent eyes.

But these were things she didn't need reminding of. Zuhal's allure and charisma had never been in any doubt. It was his other qualities she needed to remember right now. His ruthlessness and determination. His ability to cast something aside once he was bored with it. She needed to remind herself that she had simply been a diversion. A sexual plaything to amuse himself with before the time came to take a suitable bride.

There was no conventional greeting from him—no pleasant social niceties which other men might have felt duty-bound to make. He walked straight past her and, without warning or ceremony, slapped a Manila envelope down on the table before turning to look at her, his black eyes glittering. 'You might want to read this before we go any further,' he observed.

'What is it?' she questioned.

He hesitated—an uncharacteristic enough gesture for Jasmine to instantly be on her guard.

'In a nutshell?' he responded. 'It's a legal document which requires only your signature.'

Her crushed heart crashed against her ribcage. 'My signature?' she echoed.

'That's right.'

She blinked as she surveyed the envelope

with the wariness of someone being presented with an unexploded bomb. 'What kind of legal document?'

Unbuttoning the soft leather jacket, he subjected her to the full intensity of his ebony gaze. 'One which will make you a very rich woman, Jazz,' he said quietly. 'Giving you the kind of wealth which would make creating your own fashion label a reality rather than a hopeless dream.'

'Really?' she said, trying to stop her voice from sounding as if she were being strangled but wanting—no, *needing*—to hear the full extent of his heartlessness so she could remind herself of it if ever she was stupid enough to entertain a single tender thought about him. 'And what exactly would I have to do to get this money?'

There was a pause.

'I think you know the answer to that. You sign over all rights to my son.'

She'd known he was going to say something on those lines but she hadn't expected his statement to be quite so bald. It was shocking and it was unbelievable. In effect he was asking her to *sell her baby*! To sign over 'all rights' to him and make as if she hadn't grown in her womb for nine whole months before he'd finally flopped, red-faced and bawling, into the world, after a long labour which had had her screaming with pain and gripping onto the hand of the nearest midwife, because she had birthed Darius alone.

She remembered the kick of his little heel against her distended belly during the long, hot summer of her pregnancy. The sight of his little heart fluttering frantically during the ultrasound appointments at the hospital, when she had blinked at the rapidly moving image and thought how it seemed like magic. Could he really be asking her to just give her son up, to hand him over for an inflated sum of money?

She searched his face for some sign that he might feel bad about making his brutal request, but there was no guilt or shame on his hawk-like features. Nothing other than a grim determination to get what he wanted, as befitted an all-powerful sheikh. And even though she wanted to fly across the room and rake her fingernails down that hard face while demanding to know how he dared to be so cruel and ruthless, Jasmine resisted the urge to retaliate in anything other than a calm and rea-

soned manner. Because drama wouldn't serve
her well. In fact, it wouldn't surprise her if he
had one of his palace doctors listening at the
door recording their conversation, waiting for
the first opportunity to pronounce her as hysterical and unfit to care for the baby prince.
A new determination began to rise up inside
her, made stronger by her fierce and protec-
tive love for her little boy. 'You must know
I could never agree to that, Zuhal,' she said,
equally quietly.

He subjected her to an assessing look. 'I
had hoped you might be reasonable, Jazz.' The
tightening of his jaw was the only outward
sign that he was irritated by her response. 'But
if you really think that maintaining contact
across two such dramatically different cul-
tures would benefit the child's welfare, rather
than unsettling the hell out of him—then we
will have to negotiate some sort of visitation
rights for you.'

Some sort of visitation rights? Had he taken
leave of his senses? Jasmine stared at him in
confusion before comprehension dawned on
her and she gave a sudden laugh. 'Oh, I see,'
she said slowly. 'That's the first rule of successful bargaining, isn't it? You go in high,

then negotiate down. You make your initial proposition so outlandish that I'm then supposed to be grateful for every little concession you make afterwards. Isn't that right? But we aren't talking about oil or diamonds or territory here, Zuhal, or any of the things you usually bargain for—we're talking about a baby.' The breath felt thick and tight in her throat. She felt as if she could hardly get the words out. 'I'm not going to just hand him over to you and *visit* him! Apart from missing him more than I can imagine—I wouldn't put it past you to veto my visa and ban me from ever entering Razrastan! How can you possibly ask such a thing and claim to have any humanity in your heart? Every child needs its mother!'

Zuhal met her furious glare. She was wrong about that, he thought bitterly. No child *needed* a mother. He had managed well enough without his, hadn't he? Even though the Queen had been there *physically*—a glamorous and ethereal presence in the royal palace—she had never been there for him. Shamelessly devoted to his older brother, she had taken parental favouritism and elevated it to a whole new level. Many times he had thought it would be preferable growing up without her, for she used to look through him as if he were invisible. She had made him *feel* invisible.

'Having a mother isn't *necessary*,' he bit out. 'Many successful men and women have managed perfectly well without a maternal influence. You have only to examine the pages of history to realise that.'

In frustration she shook her head and a lock of buttery blonde hair fell against her flushed cheek. 'I'm not talking about mothers who die or who for some reason can't look after their children. I'm talking about mothers who have a choice. And I do have a choice, Zuhal. Oh, I may not have your money or power but I have something which is worth a whole lot more than any of those things, and that is love. I love Darius with all my heart and I would do anything for him. Anything. And I can tell you right now that, no matter what you say or try to do, you won't succeed in taking him away from me!'

Zuhal's eyes narrowed as he absorbed the passionate fervour of her words. She was daring to argue with him in a way she would never have done in the past, when her role in his life had been nothing more than his compliant mistress, whose role had been to bring him pleasure. She had become a lioness during their separation, he realised with grudging admiration, before wondering how he was going to talk her out of her convictions.

Once it would have been easy. A soft smile and seeking look would have been enough to get her to capitulate to his wishes. But back then their roles had been very different and no one would ever have described them as equals. And things had changed. She'd just told him she had no power but she was wrong. She had all the power because she had his son and it seemed he was going to have to move strategically to get what he wanted.

Taking a few moments' respite from the unresolved thoughts which were racing around his mind, he looked around her cramped cottage, registering again how cheap it looked. For the first time it occurred to him that, despite her earlier promise to 'rustle up' some food, there was no evidence of this. No table lovingly set with candles or flowers. No napkin elaborately folded to resemble a fan or some other such nonsense. In short, none of the lavish attention to detail he was used to whenever he had allowed a woman to cook for him.

'I mean what I say, Zuhal,' she continued, her terse words falling into the uneasy silence which had fallen. 'You're not rubbing me out of Darius's life and behaving as if I didn't exist.'

Turning away from his scrutiny of the decor, he fixed her with a steady stare. 'The alternative will not be easy,' he warned softly.

She blinked with incomprehension. 'What do you mean?'

'Having a child being brought up as half-royal, half-commoner. Half-English and half-Razrastanian.'

'Then let him be brought up as English.'

'No way,' he growled. 'He needs to be aware of his royal ancestry and the responsibilities which might one day rest upon his shoulders.'

She frowned at him. 'Surely you're not implying that Darius could one day be King—when he is illegitimate.'

Zuhal stilled as a sudden wave of cynical possibility washed over him. Was this what she had secretly hoped for all along? he wondered. She'd accused him of going in with high stakes, but perhaps she was doing the same thing in her determination to drive a hard bargain. Perhaps the reality was that she was ambitious for herself as well as for her son. Perhaps having had a little time to think about it, she was imagining what could be hers, if she went about it in the right way. Because what woman wouldn't want to be a queen of the desert, with jewels and palaces and unrivalled wealth? More than that, who wouldn't want to be married to *him*? Many had jockeyed for that position in the past, but none had succeeded.

'If you're trying to get me to marry you, I can tell you right now it's not going to happen.' His voice took on a harsh and forbidding note. 'Because nothing has changed, Jazz. You are still a foreign divorcee who would be totally unsuitable for the role of Queen. My people would never accept you. Which is why I must put duty first and continue my search to find a suitable bride. But that doesn't mean that Darius can't be my insurance policy—just in case I don't produce another male heir.'

Her look of quiet reflection was replaced by one of incredulity. 'Trying to get you to marry me?' she scoffed. 'Do you really think I'd want to marry a man who treats women like second-class citizens—who regards his little boy as nothing but an *insurance policy*?'

'Fortunately, that question is destined to remain academic, since I have no intention of doing so.' His smile was swift and dismissive. 'Which means we must come to an alternative arrangement which will satisfy all parties.'

'What kind of arrangement?' Defiantly, she tilted her chin. 'What do you want?'

There was a pause. 'Who knows his true identity?'

'Nobody—not even my cousin,' she answered truthfully. 'I couldn't see the point of people finding out his father was a sheikh.'

He nodded. 'Good.'

'I didn't do it in order to get your praise,' she objected. 'I did it because I wanted to be able to trust people's true motives for getting to know us. I didn't want us to stand out, or for Darius to be made into a talking point.'

'If my brother had not died then things would be very different,' he observed reflectively. 'But he did. One day I hope to have a legitimate heir, but if that doesn't happen, then Darius will be entitled to inherit the crown. And since you refuse to let me take him back to Razrastan, then it seems he must grow up here. With you.'

'Well, thank heavens for that,' she said,

breathing out a sigh of relief. 'Because I can't think of anything worse for his welfare than being incarcerated in some gilded palace with an autocratic brute like you!'

His nostrils flared. 'Nobody else would dare speak to me in such a way,' he iced out.

'That's about the only piece of information which has given me pleasure during this entire meeting!'

'Enough!' he snapped. 'It is imperative Darius learns about the country he might one day rule, which is why I want him brought up in London, so he can be schooled at the Razrastanian embassy. In a city which is big, and anonymous. Where nobody is going to discover his true identity—not if you don't tell them.'

'But we don't live in London, Zuhal,' she pointed out. 'We live in Oxfordshire.'

'That is not a problem. You will move.'

'I am not a pawn on a chessboard! I will not move!'

His patience seemingly exhausted, he slammed his fist down on a flimsy-looking table which shivered beneath the force and when he looked at her, Jasmine could see a fire-like determination blazing from his black eyes.

'I will take no more of your futile arguments, Jazz—or your defiant show of so-called pride in refusing to accept my support,' he raged. 'Because there are some things you need to understand. And number one is that there is no way a royal prince will be brought up somewhere like this! Why, there is barely room to swing a cat!'

'We don't have a cat.'

'Will you stop interrupting me?' he raged. 'You will need to be rehoused somewhere befitting my son's status. Somewhere secure.' His gaze moved with withering precision to the crack in the peeling window-frame, which was currently sending a whistle of chilly air into the small room. 'A place which isn't offering an open invitation for thieves and has room for the bodyguards our son needs and which I will be providing, whether you like it or not. Money is obviously not a consideration and I imagine you will quickly discover that you'll enjoy living somewhere which is considerably different from this.' His mouth hardened into a cynical line. 'Most women find luxury addictive, in my experience.'

Jasmine felt a mixture of fury and pain—and his reference to the other women in his life wasn't helping matters. He was insulting her home and lifestyle and maybe she should take him to task for that. But couldn't part of her see the wisdom in what he said, much as she hated to admit it? The modest savings she'd accrued while working at the Granchester hadn't lasted nearly as long as she'd expected, and her sewing only brought in enough money for them to keep their heads above water. Life was often a struggle and it was only going to get worse. She knew what it was like to be the poor kid in school. The one who was forced to sign up for free school dinners. Who lived in fear of someone commenting about the too-small hand-me-down clothes or the shoes which badly needed heeling. The last thing she wanted was for Darius to grow up like that—so how could she let pride stand in the way?

She gave a reluctant shrug. 'I suppose what you say makes sense.'

Zuhal's eyes narrowed. It was not the gratitude he had expected—not by any stretch of the imagination. He inclined his head with regal solemnity, but behind the formal mask he seethed at her stubbornness and thanklessness. 'I will have my people arrange somewhere for you to live as soon as possible,' he said coolly. 'Just pack up the essentials and be ready to leave when you hear from my office.'

Again, she was shaking her head, the long plait swinging like a blonde pendulum, and Zuhal was suddenly filled with an urgent desire to see her newly long hair spread out over his pillow.

'Actually, I would prefer to have some choice in our new home,' she said.

He opened his mouth as if to object, before closing it again. 'Very well,' he agreed reluctantly. 'I will have a shortlist drawn up for you to consider. And you'll need a new wardrobe—not just for the baby, but for you.'

She gave a bitter laugh. 'I don't want your charity, Zuhal. I never did. I'll wear what I always wear and make my own clothes.'

'You will do no such thing,' he contradicted icily. 'Because you are no longer a shopworker living in hotel accommodation, or a single mother struggling to get by. You will be living in an expensive part of the city and it will naturally arouse suspicion if you look out of place—which, given your current appearance, wouldn't be difficult.'

Jasmine might have objected if his words

hadn't been painfully true. She'd always tried to keep herself looking nice but it wasn't as easy as it had been in the past. Darius took up a lot of her waking hours and there simply wasn't the time to make new outfits for herself. Or the money. She tucked a long strand of hair behind her ear. It was why she'd stopped going to the hairdresser—why she'd let her trademark bob grow out.

She chewed her lip. It would be awful if she refused Zuhal's charity—because that was essentially what it was—and then got mistaken for a cleaner or a nanny when she was stepping into the elevator in her smart new London home. Because she knew how money worked. She'd worked at the Granchester long enough to recognise that rich people were only really comfortable with people like themselves. Who looked like them and spoke like them. And she didn't. Not by any stretch of the imagination. Not in her cheap jeans and a thrift shop sweater from which no amount of washing could shift the stubborn stain of regurgitated carrot purée which sat on the shoulder like a faded epaulet.

And then something else occurred to her. 'What about you?' she questioned.

He had been gathering up the Manila envelope which he had dumped on the table on his arrival but he looked up when she spoke, his black eyes watchful. 'What about me?'

'Where will you be living?'

He shrugged. 'I shall make sure I have a base in London close enough to see my son, but for the rest of the time I shall be in Razrastan, preparing for my future. For the formal signing of government papers to allow me to rule until...' his voice faltered slightly '...until my brother can be legally declared dead.'

She nodded, forcing herself to remember the human tragedy which lay at the heart of all this. 'Of course,' she said, sympathy softening her voice despite his harshness towards her.

There was a pause. He seemed to hesitate. 'And of course, I have another important matter to consider.'

'Oh? What's that?'

'My marriage,' he stated coolly.

Jasmine started, her heart jolting as if someone had just pulsed an electric shock right through it. 'Your marriage?'

He nodded. 'I still need someone by my side to help me rule my country—and as soon as possible. Which is why I must find a suitable candidate. I just wanted to warn you in advance, in case the press start speculating.' His gaze seared over her like a dark laser. 'I know what you're thinking, Jazz. That the discovery of my son and heir is a complicating factor in my matrimonial plans, but I don't anticipate any problems.' He smiled. 'My future wife will need to be a very understanding woman, for that is one of my requirements. And during access visits, she will love our son and treat him as her own. I will make sure of that.'

Jasmine prayed her face wouldn't betray her feelings. Had he really said he knew what she was thinking? He didn't have a *clue*. The hurt. The anger. The shame. The *fear*. She told herself she didn't care what Zuhal did with his life or who he took as his wife. But she did. Of course she did. She wanted to rail against the thought of another woman becoming stepmother to Darius, but there wasn't a lot she could do about it. It was a fact of modern life. She'd had a stepmother herself, hadn't she?

And look how that had turned out. Her father's much younger wife had resented all evidence that he'd been married before. She hadn't even allowed Jasmine to play with her baby stepsister—though that had actually worked in everyone's favour, because Jasmine's mother had been hysterical at the thought her daughter might prefer her new 'blended' family.

Painful memories of the past dissolved and Jasmine met the ebony ice of Zuhal's stare. She wished she could tell him to go to hell and that she had no intention of letting him move her into an apartment in a strange city, no matter how luxurious it happened to be. But she couldn't do that, because she recognised that Zuhal wanted the best for his son and maybe anonymous London was a better option than a rural little village. But that didn't mean that she had to roll over like a puppy dog and accept whatever he was prepared to throw her way, did it? Which meant she didn't have to entertain him for a second longer than she needed to. This man who was impervious to her pain.

'Would you like to look in on Darius before you leave?' she questioned in a calm voice, slightly mollified by his look of bemusement.

'Leave?' He frowned. 'Weren't you supposed to be cooking me supper?'

Her expression didn't change. 'There's nothing on the go, I'm afraid. But even if there was, I seem to have lost my appetite. And quite frankly, you're the last person I feel like sharing a meal with right now, Zuhal.'

CHAPTER FOUR

'So.' Zuhal's deep voice was clipped and matter-of-fact. 'What do you think of your new home?'

Jasmine wasn't sure what to think. She was still whirling from the speed with which her move to London had happened, and, with Darius now fast asleep in his luxury new baby seat, this was the first chance she'd had to get her bearings since arriving in the city that morning. To get used to her new accommodation. Home, Zuhal had called it—yet it didn't feel a bit like home.

She glanced around the sitting room—trying to get used to a room the size of a football pitch, with its stunning views over the bright green treetops of Hyde Park. It was the place she'd liked best out of the shortlist of properties the Sheikh's office had drawn up, mainly because it was the only one which didn't make her feel as if she was hemmed in by other buildings. This high up the traffic was just a distant hum—like bees—so it almost felt as if you were in the country rather than in the middle of a city. Jasmine had seen the apartment when it had been empty and cavernous—but in the interim, it had been completely and luxuriously furnished by an unknown hand.

She would have liked some say in the furniture herself and although she couldn't fault the decor, it had a distinctly impersonal feel to it—as if some top-end designer had simply thrown a lot of money at it. Giant velvet sofas were coloured in shades echoing the soft hues of the silken rugs which adorned the gleaming wooden floors. Vibrant oil paintings hung on the pale walls and a bronze sculpture of a horse's head was silhouetted against one of the tall windows. There were even glossy unread magazines artistically placed on one of several coffee tables and coloured glass vases full of fragrant roses. It looked like a set from a film—a room designed in a single day—not built up with memories, bit by bit, like a normal home. But whoever had said any of this would be normal? It wasn't normal to have been whisked here by darkened limousine,

was it? Nor to have been followed by a fleet of
bodyguards who, as far as she knew, were still
lurking outside with those suspicious-looking
lumps beneath their loose jackets.

Zuhal had arrived soon afterwards, sweeping in without any of his usual coterie of aides,
which meant she was now alone with him,
something which was making her pulse race
and her breasts to become engorged and she
hated it. She hated her body's instinctive reaction to a man who had proved how cold and
heartless he could be. Who had announced
his intention to take a royal bride and who regarded his firstborn son as his 'insurance policy'. But she was trying her best not to pass
judgement, because that wouldn't benefit Darius in the long run, would it?

She wondered if she would ever get used
to living somewhere which had three bath-
rooms—three!—all gleaming white and flashing silver and now crammed with the same
bath products she'd sold in the Granchester
Hotel boutique, so she knew exactly how eye-
watering their cost.

She had chosen her own bedroom after the
most cursory of glances because she had no
desire to be in any room containing a bed,

not with Zuhal breathing down her neck and creating the kind of flashbacks she could have happily done without. The most beautiful room of all was the nursery, which had been prepared for Darius. There was a curved crib fashioned from wood which felt satin-soft to the touch and a mobile full of planets and stars dangling from the ceiling above it. On a pristine window sill was a line of toys—fluffy bears and a soft little monkey with bright eyes. And somehow, the simple comfort of this room made Jasmine feel that the decision to move here had been the right one, if only for her son's sake.

She walked over to the window—away from the subtle sandalwood of Zuhal's scent—and peered down into the park, where she could see people braving the light spring breeze and sitting on benches to eat their supermarket sandwiches. A teenage boy was doing gravity-defying things on a skateboard. Around the line of the lake, she could see the yellow blur of daffodils, all dancing and fluttering in the breeze—just like in the poem she'd learnt at school. She'd been hopeful back then—until her mother's final meltdown about her father's supposed sins had made schooling something she'd just had to fit in whenever she could, and attention to homework an impossible dream.

But something about that memory made her think about the future. Her own ambitions might have tumbled along the wayside, but Darius still had a lifetime to look forward to. Shouldn't she try to put a positive spin on everything which was happening, despite her many misgivings? To answer the Sheikh's question with enthusiasm rather than doubt.

'It's lovely,' she said, as she turned back to face him.

If he had been expecting a slightly more ringing endorsement, he made no reference to it. 'And do you think you can be happy here?' he persisted.

Happy? It was a funny question. Since Darius's birth, all Jasmine had wanted was to ensure security for him and now she'd done just that—even though she hadn't planned it. From now on the two of them were going to be living in unbelievable splendour, while Zuhal picked up all the bills. She should have been relieved, and yet…

How could she possibly be relieved—or relaxed—when part of her still wanted the Sheikh so badly, even though she knew it was wrong to feel that way? Her body ached whenever he was in the vicinity and she was poignantly reminded of how it had felt when he used to make love to her, and a big part of her wanted that to happen all over again. Yet he'd blithely told her he was going in search of a bride who would one day become her baby's stepmother. Wouldn't that kind of cold cruelty fill most people with anger instead of desire?

Unwillingly, she began to study him—wondering if she would be able to do that objectively. But for now, at least, objectivity was a fruitless expectation. His dark grey suit flattered his broad-shouldered body to perfection, subtly showcasing all the muscular power which lay beneath. He had been born to make women look at him, with those hawkish good looks and eyes of ebony fire. She remembered the way she used to stroke her fingers through his hair—giving him the Indian head massage which one of the spa therapists at the Granchester had taught her to do. She remembered what an overdeveloped feeling of pleasure it had given her—to have the powerful and alpha Sheikh purring like a pussycat and relaxing under her rhythmical ministrations.

With an effort she dragged her gaze away

from him and glanced out of the window, where sunlight was bouncing off the fresh green leaves which were shimmering in the distance. 'I'm going to do everything in my power to be happy,' she said truthfully.

'Good. That is the kind of positive attitude I like.'

She shrugged as she turned to meet his eyes. 'I'm not doing it for your benefit, Zuhal. I owe it to my son.'

'Our son, Jazz. Please don't ever forget that,' he corrected smoothly, shooting a quick glance at his watch as the doorbell rang, its peal sounding unnaturally loud as it echoed through the spacious apartment. 'Excellent. Right on cue. Come with me, please.'

Jasmine blinked. Surely they weren't expecting visitors? During several heated debates about privacy during the choosing of this apartment, she'd got the definite message that she and Zuhal weren't going to be doing any socialising together. In fact, their relationship—such as it was—was very definitely to be kept under the radar. Which suited her just fine. She wanted to spend as little time with him as possible. No. Why not put it another way? She *needed* to spend as little time with him as possible, if she wanted to hang onto her sanity. 'Come where?' she questioned. 'Who's that ringing the doorbell?'

'Wait and see.'

Jasmine clamped her lips shut, annoyed at his high-handedness but, her curiosity alerted, she followed him past the blissfully sleeping Darius, towards the front door.

After a low-voiced command in his native tongue, the door was opened from the outside by a bodyguard, to reveal a woman standing there. Aged around thirty, she was dressed in what Jasmine recognised instantly as traditional Razrastanian robes and her hair was coiled on top of her head in an elaborate fretwork of black waves. She directed a kind smile towards Jasmine before bobbing a curtsey to Zuhal, who immediately indicated that she should stand at ease as he gestured for her to enter the apartment.

'Jazz, I'd like you to meet Rania,' he said. 'She is going to be helping you look after Darius. His new nanny.'

'I am very pleased to meet you, mistress,' said Rania in perfectly modulated English. 'And I am very much looking forward to meeting Darius.'

'Why don't you come and meet him right now?' suggested Zuhal smoothly.

'He's asleep,' said Jasmine quickly, still reeling from this latest development and yet another demonstration of Zuhal's high-handedness.

'I will not wake him, mistress,' said Rania softly.

What else could she do other than lead her to the baby? Jasmine told herself it was pitiful how hard her heart clenched as she watched the Razrastanian woman crouch down and fix her dark gaze on the sleeping Darius, as if committing every atom to memory.

'The son of the Sheikh is a truly magnificent baby,' said Rania at last, as she straightened up.

Jasmine couldn't fault the sentiment but her smile felt forced. She felt like a puppet. As if everyone were pulling her strings. Moving her this way, then that—leaving her with no idea of where she was or what she was doing. And all she could think of were the words Rania had spoken and which were now circling inside her head. *The son of the Sheikh. The son of the Sheikh.* Was the Razrastanian nanny, despite her kind smile and soft voice, planning to push Jasmine to the side-lines and edge her out of the picture, so that his royal father could assume complete dominance? She could feel her mouth growing firm with determination. Well, that was never going to happen.

Never.

'He bears such a strong resemblance to his father,' Rania was cooing.

Jasmine wished she could deny it. To say that, actually, the baby had *her* eyes or *her* hair—but there was no evidence of her features, or her hazel eyes or blonde locks. With his olive skin and black hair, there surely couldn't be another child on the planet who was more a mini-me of his darkly handsome father than Darius. His limbs were sturdy, his eyelashes outrageously long, and the baby clinic had already told her how tall he was going to be.

'Indeed he is, Rania,' Jasmine said, trying to regain her composure as she turned her attention to more practical matters. 'Where-abouts…um, where will you be staying?'

She could see Rania looking uncertainly towards Zuhal as if for guidance and the Sheikh interposed instantly.

'Rania has her own apartment, which is con-nected to this one,' he said, with the smooth assurance of a man who had thought of everything. 'I don't think you can have paid it very much attention during your first viewing.'

Jasmine's lips tightened. Obviously not.

'I was here yesterday, putting the final touches to it,' said Rania proudly. 'Would you care to see it, mistress?'

'I most certainly would,' said Jasmine, shooting Zuhal a furious glance. 'And really, there's no need to call me mistress. Jasmine will do just fine.'

'But—'

'*Please*,' said Jasmine firmly, wondering if Rania—despite all her linguistic skill—had any idea that the word mistress had a very different meaning in English. One which she definitely did not wish to be associated with *her*. She forced a new brightness into her voice. 'Let's go, shall we? I can't wait to see where you'll be living, Rania.'

In silence, the three of them walked along the long corridor, until they reached a door at the far end, which Jasmine hadn't noticed before. Or rather, it was the one thing the agent hadn't bothered to point out during an otherwise extensive tour—perhaps if she'd been feeling a little less dazed she might have discovered it herself. The Razrastanian woman pushed open the door and gestured for them to step inside, which Jasmine did—although she noticed that Zuhal remained standing broodily on the threshold.

Inside, was a separate and very beautiful little apartment, with a door leading to a bedroom and another to a neat kitchen. A sitting room with its own small terrace overlooked the park and on one of the walls was a framed poster of a place Jasmine instantly recognised. She felt as if someone were twisting a knife inside her as she studied the imposing building in the foreground of the picture. A golden palace with soaring towers and cobalt cupolas which glinted in the bright sunshine. Jasmine swallowed, for she knew that this was Zuhal's home. The home he would soon share with his royal bride.

And, for half the year—with Darius, too.

'What a beautiful view you've got, Rania,' she said weakly.

Did Zuhal guess how churned up she was feeling? Was that why he stepped forward, to take her by the elbow to support her, as if she were an old lady he was helping to cross a busy road. Quickly she brushed his hand away because she didn't want him touching her—and not just because she couldn't trust her body's reaction to him. Did he really think that an outward show of concern could make up for the fact that he was behaving like an overbearing brute? First, he'd announced that he intended marrying another woman—and now this!

'Why don't we let Rania get settled in?' he suggested smoothly. 'You can both talk baby routine later.'

Rania nodded, quietly closing the door as she disappeared into her rooms, and Jasmine waited until she and Zuhal were back in the sitting room before she said anything. Waited until they were completely out of earshot and made sure that Darius was still asleep—and that her breathing had settled down-so her words didn't come out in a senseless babble.

'You let me vet the apartment!' she accused him hotly. 'But you didn't think to give me the opportunity of telling you whether or not I liked the woman you have employed to help take care of our son?'

'Everyone likes Rania,' he said.

'That's not the point!' Dangerously close to yelling, Jasmine sucked in a deep, unsteady breath. 'And what's more—you know it! So don't give me that *I don't know what you're talking about* look and expect me to be taken in by it!'

Zuhal found himself taken aback by her rage and, in another situation, might almost have been amused by it—because didn't such passion always change into something much more agreeable when it was transferred to the bedroom? But that was never going to happen, judging by the way Jazz was glaring at him— with emerald fire spitting from her eyes.

Undeterred, he loosened his tie a fraction. 'He is a desert prince, Jazz,' he said. 'And having a nanny is a given for all royal children. He will be looked after by someone who speaks my language and who knows the myths and legends of my country. He will grow up bilingual, which is essential for a boy who might one day be King.'

'But I've only ever looked after him myself. I told you before—I've never left him with a stranger.'

'Rania is the daughter of my own nanny at the palace—my favourite, as it happens. She speaks perfect English and received her training at one of the finest establishments in England, one which provides childcare for your own royal family, just in case you're interested.'

'Not particularly. And that isn't the point. You should have asked me first.'

His patience was beginning to wear thin but Zuhal bit back the impatient retort which was on the tip of his tongue, telling himself to go easy on her. To treat her with impartiality as they negotiated their way through these tricky new waters. But how was such impartiality possible when his mind and his body had been in constant conflict, since he'd walked up the weed-strewn path of her little cottage less than a fortnight ago? When every night since he had been plagued by memories of her soft breasts and curvy hips. By the disturbing recall of the way she used to wriggle over his body like some kind of sexy eel, mounting him with a yelp of exultant pleasure as she rode them both to fulfilment. And then afterwards run her fingers through his hair, digging their firm tips into his scalp and massaging away the tension, so that he'd been left feeling almost *boneless* with pleasure.

The other day he'd kissed her and the kiss they'd shared had been as potent as any he could remember. Was that because it had been abruptly cut short and not allowed to proceed to its natural conclusion? Was that why his subsequent sense of frustration had been more pronounced than any he could remember? Zuhal acknowledged the hard jerk of his groin, feeling as if his body was somehow taunting him.

There were a million reasons why he shouldn't want her, even if you discounted her basic unsuitability. She had deceived him. Had tried to keep their child a secret from him. Why, even when Darius had cried out, when he had still been ignorant of his identity, Zuhal had seen the distress clouding her pale face—and then her deliberate manipulation as she had sought to distract him.

If she could have got him out of her cottage without disclosing he was a father, then she would have done, he reminded himself grimly.

But even that knowledge did not lessen her allure, or stop him from wishing he could carry her into one of those conveniently empty bedrooms to slake his hunger for her, once and for all. And then maybe rid her memory from his mind for ever.

He sighed. Compromise wasn't something

he was often called upon to use, but maybe he should make an exception in this case. Slowly he inclined his head, determined to acknowledge her concerns. 'If, for any reason, Rania proves unsatisfactory...' he saw her visibly brighten '...any *sensible* reason,' he added swiftly, 'then we can use someone else. Do you think I would do anything to threaten or disrupt the life of my son, Jazz?'

'Now you're making me sound unreasonable.'

'That was not my intention. Darius needs someone in his life other than his parents,' he said. 'Someone to trust and feel safe with. Surely you must see that?'

She was nodding her head now, as if determined to match his own mood of compromise with one of her own. Smoothing her dress down with fingers he noticed weren't quite steady, she met his eyes with a rare expression of complicity. 'I suppose you're right.' She shrugged. 'Especially since he doesn't have any grandparents.'

Zuhal's mouth hardened, but he was unable to manufacture any sorrow that this was the case, for he had grown up without knowing his own grandparents, which might have helped dissolve some of the tensions which had existed in the palace. But he had survived, hadn't he? Deliberately, he focussed his gaze on Jazz because that was infinitely more pleasurable than thinking about the toxic environment in which he had been raised.

In just a fortnight the chill weather had turned into something more usual for this time of year and her simple cotton dress was sprigged with blossom—she had clearly made it herself—with her soft pink cardigan a shade lighter than the tiny flowers. She looked young, vibrant and utterly desirable and Zuhal was filled with a powerful desire to touch her. To crush his lips down on hers and to slide his fingers beneath her floaty skirt and touch her where she was warm and sticky. His throat thickened. Yet despite the undeniable allure of her appearance, she looked like a student on her way to lectures, not a young woman who now occupied one of the most expensive pieces of real estate in London.

'I thought I told you to buy yourself some new clothes,' he observed.

'What's wrong with what I'm wearing?'

'There's nothing *wrong* with them. But your clothes are not appropriate for your new position in life, Jazz,' he said softly. 'We both know that.'

She gave a quick nod of her head, as if she was preparing to say something difficult. 'And how exactly would you define that position, Zuhal—that's something we haven't discussed, have we?'

Zuhal tensed. Was this an invitation to be completely frank with her? To reach a new understanding which they could both enjoy to the max? What was it the English sometimes said? *To make hay while the sun shines.* He felt his pulse quicken. Her eyes were no longer flashing green fire, obscuring the golden lights which usually glinted there. But in place of the anger he could detect a distinct smokiness—and Zuhal had known enough women to recognise what that meant. Hadn't she made it obvious when he'd walked in here today and looked at him with desire in her eyes? When he had observed the instinctive hardening of her nipples beneath the cheap cotton of her dress.

'That's up to you, Jazz,' he said silkily. 'The decision is yours.'

Her eyes narrowed with suspicion. 'You're being very…oblique. I'm still not quite sure what you mean.'

'Then let me state my words plainly, so there can be no misunderstanding.' He paused, aware that his throat had dried, so that it resembled the dust of his beloved desert homeland. 'When we kissed the other day, there was no doubt that the passion which burns between us was as strong as before. I looked at you and I wanted you. I still do, despite your determination to keep my son from me and your subsequent defiant behaviour. But I am willing to overlook your stubbornness, because you were the best lover I've ever had.' He glittered her a smile. 'And I am eager to taste such pleasures with you again.'

She nodded her head solemnly, as if she was giving his words careful thought before responding to them. 'You're saying you want us to take up where we left off last time, is that it?'

He slanted her a smile. The kind of smile which women had told him was like being caught beneath the full force of the sun. 'I couldn't have put it better myself,' he said softly.

'Even though you are currently in the market for a royal bride?'

His smile died. 'That isn't going to happen

overnight, Jazz. Even though speed is of the essence—I don't anticipate taking a wife before the end of the year.'

'And during that brief window of opportunity, we'll be lovers?'

'I knew you would understand,' he breathed.

'Oh, I understand all right.' The fire in her eyes was back and so too was the mulish tilt of her chin. 'I understand that you're an arrogant man with an overdeveloped sense of entitlement, who treats women like toys he can just pick up and toss away once he's had enough of them.'

She took a step closer, like a boxer squaring up to an opponent in the ring.

'Do you really think I'm going to hang around here, waiting for one of your rare visits—ready to drop everything when you deign to show your face-and then simply fall into bed with you?'

'How dare you speak to me this way?'

'While in the meantime,' she continued remorselessly, 'you're out there courting every eligible princess the desert region has to offer in order to find yourself a suitable bride?'

'That's a very extreme way of looking at it,' he bit out.

'It's the truth, Zuhal,' she said. 'What other way is there to look at it?'

He glowered at her. 'I have been completely straight with you, Jazz. Perhaps you would do me the honour of returning the favour. And if you don't want to be my lover, then how do you intend spending your time?'

Jasmine sucked in a deep breath, knowing she needed to be strong. Or at least she needed to *appear* strong. Zuhal didn't have to know she wanted intimacy just as much as he did—the difference being that for her it spelt emotional danger. 'You are planning to live your life as you see fit, Zuhal,' she said quietly. 'And I'm going to do exactly the same. I'm going to be the best mother I can, and to accommodate your wishes where Darius is concerned. But I'm also going to live my own life. I plan to make friends and forge a future for myself.'

'With a man?' he shot out instantly.

Jasmine couldn't deny the pleasure she got from the dark look of jealousy which crossed his features and made his shadowed jaw clench. And although the thought of being anywhere near any man other than Zuhal made her feel violently sick, he didn't have to know that.

'Who knows what I will do? I'm young and free and single,' she said, with a carelessness she hoped didn't sound faked. 'And this is England, Zuhal. Where men and women are equal.'

He gave an angry snort, a pulse flickering wildly at his temple as he walked away without another word, and Jasmine was surprised that the loud slamming of the front door hadn't woken the baby.

CHAPTER FIVE

'HIS ROYAL HIGHNESS is waiting for you in the drawing room, mistress.'

Pausing in the middle of unbuckling Darius from a buggy the size of a small car, Jasmine hid her frown as she was met by a nervous-looking Rania. She'd learnt it was pointless to ask the nanny not to call her 'mistress', just as she'd learnt she had absolutely no control over the Sheikh's movements in her life. That he turned up when he felt like it and, of course, could walk right in whenever he wanted to because there was always Rania or a body-guard to let him in. And because he owned it, of course. She might be the one who was living here, but Zuhal was the one who had paid for the apartment and everything it contained. Sometimes it felt as if he *owned* her, too.

It wasn't an ideal situation, because every time he arrived she had to fight an instinctive urge to touch him—and how crazy was *that*? Just as she had to fight the desire to stare at him and drink in all his power and his hard, masculine beauty—because remembering just how good it felt to be in his arms would do her no favours at all. He flew into London once a week on business and Jasmine tried to make herself scarce whenever he arrived to see his son, although Rania was always on hand to meekly obey his orders. Because pretending they were a happy family was nothing but a mockery of the harsh reality.

And because she didn't want to get stuck into a doomed pattern of togetherness, which would be shattered when he found himself a royal bride.

But every time Zuhal left, she had to go through the process of eradicating him from her mind, telling herself that meaningless sex with her ex-lover was a bad idea in every respect, no matter how much her body craved it or how fierce the unspoken attraction which always seemed to sizzle between them. She'd had her chance and she'd done the right thing in turning it down. That ship had sailed.

Rania stepped forward. 'Let me take Darius for you, mistress.'

'Thanks, Rania—but I'll do it. I think he's teething because he was up for most of the night. He was a bit cranky in the clinic this morning, but the nurse said he's coming on leaps and bounds.'

Nervously, Rania cleared her throat. 'This is excellent news, mistress, but His Royal Highness will not enjoy being kept waiting.'

'I'm sure he won't,' said Jasmine, a renewed cheerfulness washing over her, despite her lack of sleep. 'But maybe it will do him good.'

'You think so?' A silken voice came filtering through the air and Jasmine felt all the little hairs on the back of her neck prickling in anticipation as Zuhal entered the hallway with noiseless stealth. She could sense his presence with every soft footstep he took towards her and it took a moment for her to compose herself so that her expression would register indifference, rather than desire. She looked up to meet his gleaming eyes as, pausing only to trace the tip of a finger over his son's soft cheek, he turned to the Razrastanian nanny. 'Rania, will you mind taking care of Darius so that I can speak to Jazz in private?'

'Certainly, Your Royal Highness.'

Eagerly, Rania complied, removing Darius from his buggy with the tender efficiency which Jasmine had grown to like and trust—although she didn't like the way the nanny always deferred to the Sheikh. She looked down at the baby's black curls with a rush of fierce, maternal love, but her heart sank a little as Zuhal gestured for her to accompany him to the sitting room, where, outside, the spring flowers in the park had given way to the bright blooms of early summer.

'You didn't think to warn me that you were coming?' she said, bending down to unnecessarily straighten a velvet cushion which the cleaner had placed at perfect right angles to the one beside it.

'Why would I do that?' he questioned blandly. 'Unless you were planning to do something which you know would anger me, should I walk in on you unexpectedly. Is that the case, Jazz?'

'Please don't talk in riddles, because I haven't got the energy to work them out, Zuhal,' she said. 'Like what?'

'Like being here with another man,' he accused, all blandness gone now as a cold note of steel entered his voice.

'I don't know what you're talking about.'

'I think you do.' He began to pace the room, more agitated than she'd ever seen him. 'There was a man here yesterday.'

Jasmine narrowed her eyes as memory came flooding back to her. 'How on earth do you know that?'

'How do you think I know?' he demanded. 'Because my bodyguards informed me!'

'So you're having me *spied* on now, are you?' she returned. 'Bad enough you sent someone to investigate the playgroup I decided to join—as if I wasn't capable of making a judgement about it myself—but now I discover that I'm not even allowed to invite friends back to what is supposed to be my *home*, without your heavies reporting back to you!'

'Please don't be so naive, Jazz,' he hissed, his pacing footsteps coming to a halt as he turned round to fix her with a blistering stare. 'My son is currently under your care and naturally my staff keep me informed if anyone unknown to them should visit the apartment. You're lucky he wasn't stopped at the door and sent on his way. So I will ask you…who was he?'

For a moment Jasmine was tempted to call

his bluff. To tell him that the man in question was her new lover and they'd both been eagerly waiting until the baby was fast asleep so that they could jump into bed together and enjoy a wild night of passion. But there was being independent and there was being downright stupid—and no way was she going to mess with Zuhal, not when he was in this kind of mood. When a dark and dangerous anger was radiating from his powerful body in waves which were almost tangible.

Reluctantly, she shrugged. 'He's an Italian waiter I used to know when I was working at the Granchester.'

'An Italian waiter?' he repeated, as if she had just told him she'd been entertaining a mass murderer. 'What the hell was he doing here, Jazz? Practising his silver service technique, or was he teaching you how best they like to kiss in Roma?'

'Don't be so ridiculous,' she answered stiffly. 'He's actually been getting experience—'

'What kind of experience?' he shot back immediately.

'*Work* experience—before he goes back to join his father's restaurant in Lecce—not Rome,' she completed witheringly. 'His sister is pregnant and he knew I liked to sew, so he asked if I would design something especially for the new baby which he could take back to Italy with him. Which I have, although it's not quite finished. Here…' She slipped from the sitting room to one of the unused bedrooms, which she had turned into a makeshift sewing room, before returning with a tiny, hand-smocked romper suit which she waved in front of him. 'See for yourself if you don't believe me.'

As she held up the impossibly small garment, Zuhal felt the tight knot of tension which had been building up inside him dissolve—to be replaced by the instant rush of relief. Had he really imagined Jazz in the arms of another man? But that was the trouble. Of course he had. Many times. Because he was frustrated. Because he felt powerless. Because for once in his life here was a woman refusing to do what he wanted her to do, which was to fall into bed with him. He'd tried telling himself he could understand why she no longer wanted to be his lover and, as the mother of his son, her proud morality should please him. He told himself it was better all round if their relationship entered a new, platonic phase, yet still he couldn't stop thinking about her—even though logic told him that her chilly refusal to resume her tenure as his lover was only feeding his desire. That same logic had convinced him that sex was the only way to get her out of his system for good—for what woman didn't lose her allure when a man was repeatedly exposed to her?

And perhaps he was going about it the wrong way.

'I have seen something like this before,' he said slowly, his eyes still on the impossibly small garment.

'Of course you have. Darius has one which is very similar—although his is a different colour. Here I've used boats rather than ducklings.'

He nodded. 'It is an exquisite piece of work,' he said, his gaze taking in the delicate blue and white embroidery.

She was looking at him expectantly, as if waiting for the punchline. 'And?'

'And...nothing.' He shrugged, before producing a smile. 'You obviously have great talent.'

She shook her head in self-deprecating denial. 'I wouldn't go that far.'

'No arguments, Jazz. Why not just accept

the compliment in the spirit in which it was intended?'

'Okay,' she said cautiously. 'I will. Thank you.' Her cheeks a little flushed now, she regarded him warily. 'So what can I do for you today, Zuhal? Apart from giving you a platform to demonstrate your unreasonable jealousy?'

Trying not to focus on the fecund swell of her breasts, Zuhal attempted to put his jumbled thoughts into some kind of coherent order.

'There are a couple of things I need to discuss with you.'

'That's fine. Discuss away,' she said. 'But could you please do it quickly because I'm planning to take a walk in the park while the sun's still out.'

'But you've only just got back!'

'Rania will be here while Darius has his nap, so I thought I'd have a bit of a snooze in the fresh air, because your son kept me awake for a lot of the night. Forgive me for having such an outrageous plan for my afternoon—but I wasn't aware I had to clock in and out every time I left the apartment, although maybe that was stupid of me,' she added sarcastically. 'Perhaps the reason you bought the whole penthouse floor of this block was because it resembles a fortress.'

'You don't like living here?' he questioned. 'This was your favourite out of the shortlist, if you remember?'

Jasmine hesitated because usually he didn't ask her opinion—riding roughshod over her wishes was much more his style. She knew she really ought to count her blessings now that she had security for her son and no financial worries. But despite these things, she'd quickly found London very different from Oxford—especially when you had a baby in tow. When she'd been working at the Granchester she'd had no responsibilities and her time off had been her own. But not any more. Now she was achingly aware that her baby needed pals his own age, which was why she had joined an infant playgroup—the one Zuhal had insisted on vetting.

Darius loved it when they sang songs and jangled tambourines and she'd met plenty of other young women her age. But they'd all been nannies, not mothers, which had made Jasmine feel even more of an outsider. She'd made friends with a couple of them on a very superficial level, but hadn't dared ask them back to her home. Because if they saw all this wall-to-wall luxury, wouldn't they inevitably start asking questions? In fact, hadn't one of them—Carrie—already tried? Questions Jasmine couldn't possibly answer because then it would all come tumbling out that she was the one-time mistress of a future king, and mother to his illegitimate heir.

'It's very comfortable,' she said, in careful reply to the Sheikh's drawled query. 'But sometimes I get stir-crazy living all the way up here. I mean, I know there's the balcony to sit on but it's not quite the same as walking outside. Sometimes I feel…'

'What?' he prompted softly.

'Oh, I don't know…' She shrugged her shoulders. 'Trapped.'

His eyes narrowed. 'I can understand that. Very well. I will grant you your wish. We will take a walk together.'

Startled, she looked at him. 'And how's that supposed to work? I thought we weren't supposed to be seen together.'

'Nobody will notice us. We will simply be a couple out walking in the sunshine, one of many such couples. My military training taught me that I can always blend into the background if I try,' he explained. 'And my bodyguards have been trained to observe from the shadows.'

Blend in?

Jasmine stared at him. Was he deluded? Dominating the vast sitting room with his powerful presence, his outward appearance wasn't so very different from the other successful businessmen who frequented this part of the capital. In his exquisitely cut charcoal suit and a silk shirt the colour of buttermilk, he was certainly dressed like your average billionaire. But he *was* different, no two ways about it. He was a desert sheikh and that affected the way he did things. The way he thought about things. She didn't particularly want to go for a walk with him yet the alternative was being cooped up inside, with the four walls closing in on them and a sensory overload on both her imagination and her body, so Jasmine nodded her head.

'Okay,' she said.

While Zuhal spoke rapidly into his cell phone in his native tongue, she went off to get ready, checking Darius and assuring Rania she wouldn't be long. Pausing only to pull on a pair of espadrilles and cram a straw hat over her head, she exited her bedroom to find Zuhal waiting for her in the hallway, looking at his golden wristwatch with ill-disguised irritation. He had removed his tie and undone the top two buttons of his shirt, offering a distracting glimpse of dark chest hair just beneath the pale silk.

Did she imagine his jaw tightening when he caught sight of the summery espadrilles whose matching pink ribbons were criss-crossed over her lower legs like a wannabe gladiator? No, she didn't think so. She might have been innocent when she met him and been subsequently accused of naivety—but she wasn't deluded enough to deny the unmistakable sensual charge which entered the atmosphere whenever they were alone together. It was the same sensory overload which made her itch to touch the slashed angles of his darkly handsome face, and to cover his lips with hungry kisses. A response which she tried her best to batten down, usually with remarkably little effect—like today—when the tug of heat low in her belly was inconveniently reminding her how big he used to feel when he was inside her.

But it was strange and curiously satisfying

being outside with him as Jasmine realised that fresh air or daylight had never really featured in their relationship. In some ways it had been more of a vampire affair. There had been those badly lit restaurants of their early dates, and afterwards her being smuggled into a borrowed mews house for snatched nights together. But the combination of blue sky and sunshine glittering on the water of the lake was making her feel curiously carefree, in a way she hadn't been for months. And Zuhal had been right about his bodyguards slipping into the shadows, because even when she looked very hard, she couldn't see them.

He hadn't exaggerated about blending in himself, either. Was it the fact that he had removed his tie, or was it just his unusually relaxed stance rather than his regal demeanour, which made him into just a spectacularly handsome man who was taking a summer stroll with his…?

What?

How would she describe her role in the future King's life? Not his girlfriend, that was for sure. Not even his lover—not any more. And mother of his child made it sound as if they'd been married, which of course they never had been. She bit her lip. She'd never had any status at all, really—which begged the question of why she had tolerated it so happily. Was that because her sexual awakening had been so powerful that it had rocked her world in a way which nothing else had come close to? Because she'd been so totally caught up in this new way of living and feeling—of being somebody's *lover*?

Or was it because at the time she'd thought herself in love with him? Crazy, really. How could you be in love with a man who treated you as a convenience—flitting in and out of your life as the mood took him? She hadn't really known him at all—and, as she was starting to get to know him now, she was seeing a ruthless side which he'd never shown before.

His deep voice broke into her reverie.

'I thought the whole point of a walk in the sunshine was that it was supposed to be relaxing, but instead you're looking as if you have all the cares of the world on your shoulders. Relax, Jazz. It's a beautiful day.'

Jasmine blinked to find the Sheikh's black gaze trained on her. The edges of his lips were curved into a smile and silently she reproached herself. She had to stop analysing stuff and wishing for things which were never going to happen. Why couldn't she just live in the moment and enjoy it?

'You're right. It is. Gorgeous.' Tilting her hat back, she breathed in, half closing her eyes until a vaguely familiar tinkle of music made her open them again. There was an ice-cream van in the distance, with a small queue of children forming at the front, and maybe it was the powerful collision between difficult past and difficult present which made something hard and hurtful coil itself around her heart.

'Jazz? Is something wrong?'

Zuhal's deep voice snapped her back to reality and she blinked at him, momentarily disconcerted. 'Why?'

'You've gone pale.' His voice had become a silken whisper. 'As pale as milk.'

If she'd been in the apartment she would never have told him, but high up in that expensive citadel, he would never have asked. And maybe that was another thing which being outside did. It freed you from inhibition. It allowed memories to rush back and with them came all the feelings, so that in that moment she was no longer a puzzled new mother, but a bewildered little girl again.

'There was an ice-cream van outside my house when I was little,' she said, her voice sounding as if it were coming from a great distance away. 'I heard the music and went outside to listen—more to drown out the sound of my parents arguing than in any great hope of getting an ice cream.'

'And did you get one?'

'Actually, I did.' She gave a quick smile, because the Sheikh's calm question meant he was able to slip almost unnoticed into her memory. 'My father came outside and bought me a cone—the biggest I'd ever seen. A massive thing heaped with pink and white ice-cream with one of those flaky chocolate bars sticking out of the top. I was surprised because he would never normally have done that and it made me wonder why he was there, in the middle of the day, when he should have been at work. He kissed me on top of my head and said goodbye in a funny kind of voice, and I remember watching him walk down the road just as my mother came flying out of the house.'

'And?' he prompted, into the silence between them, which was broken only by the far-off sound of children playing.

She shrugged. 'My mother told me he was leaving. That he had another little girl with someone else—a new daughter he loved much more than me. She said some other stuff, too—stuff I've done my best to forget—and then she had a complete meltdown. Actually, so did my ice cream,' she added flippantly as she stared at the sun-scorched grass, willing her eyes not to fill with tears. 'Amid all the drama I'd completely forgotten about it and it fell off the cornet and lay on the pavement in a big, creamy puddle.' It had been the end of her childhood and the beginning of a new and very different phase, where she had become the mother, and her mother, the child.

'Jazz,' said Zuhal softly. 'Are you crying?'

She looked up, surprised by the sudden touch of his fingertips to her face. When had he moved close enough to touch her?

'No,' she answered proudly. 'Crying is a waste of time.'

Was she imagining the gleam of understanding in his black eyes, or was it a case of just seeing what she wanted to see? A pulse began to jump at her temple as he rubbed the pad of his thumb against her chin and that simple brush of skin against hers reminded her all too vividly of the days when their bodies had lain naked together. Jasmine swallowed, praying that he would continue, knowing that if he pulled her into his arms she would not resist. Because didn't she want that? More than anything? To feel his lips on hers and be locked in his embrace, so she could let his lovemaking melt away all her pain. Wasn't she sick and tired of the celibate stand-off which had sprung up between them?

The air between them seemed to shift and change. She could feel the sudden tension in her body as he took another step towards her. A flash of hope and longing swept through her as his hawk-like features clicked into focus, when the unexpected sound of her own name made Jasmine jump back in alarm.

'Jasmine! Hey, Jasmine!'

She turned around to see Carrie, the nosy nanny from the toddler group who today had neither of her twin charges with her. She was wearing cut-off denim hot pants which made the most of what was obviously a spray tan, and a T-shirt bearing the legend *Luscious* was stretched tightly across her generous chest.

Jasmine shot a swift look at Zuhal but he wasn't ogling the brunette stunner, unlike just about every other man in the vicinity. Instead, he was regarding Carrie with an expression of cool disdain.

'Well, hi. Fancy seeing you here,' said Carrie, looking him up and down, the gleam in her eye suggesting she found his disdainful expression both a turn-on and a challenge. 'You must be Mr Jasmine?'

'This is Zuhal,' said Jasmine quickly, only to see the Sheikh glare at her. 'We were just—'

'Leaving,' said Zuhal firmly, cupping Jasmine's elbow with the guiding clasp of his palm.

'Oh.' Carrie pouted. 'Must you? I see we're all childless. Thank. The. Lord. Why don't we go over to that Pimm's tent by the bandstand? It's a perfect day for getting sloshed in the sunshine.'

'I don't drink,' said Zuhal repressively.

Jasmine thought afterwards that it was a pity Carrie took a confident step towards him because her slightly predatory action was misinterpreted as one of aggression by his phalanx of bodyguards, who immediately swarmed from behind various trees, to surround them. Carrie was blinking at them in astonishment and Jasmine noticed that one of the bodyguards was having difficulty averting his gaze from her heaving breasts.

'Oh, wow,' breathed Carrie softly. 'Now I think I'm spoilt for choice!'

The next few minutes passed in a blur. Jasmine was aware of being virtually frog-marched out of the park and back to the apartment, with Zuhal's angry words ringing in her ears. And all that softness and understanding she'd thought she'd seen in his face had vanished, replaced by a cold censure which made his eyes glint like steel.

'I cannot believe that you associate with such people!' he stormed, as the elevator zoomed them up towards the penthouse.

'I don't think she meant any harm,' she defended. 'She's just…just a young woman who likes to work hard and play hard.'

'She is a predator!' debated Zuhal fiercely. 'Who dresses like a tramp! And I do not want my son associating with someone like her— that is simply not going to happen. Do you understand, Jazz?'

'What, are you planning to vet everyone I come in contact with?'

Grimly, he nodded. 'If I need to, then yes.'

She hated the way he just breezed in and

out of her life, making changes as the mood took him, before waltzing back to Razrastan again. He needed to understand that although she was living in one of his properties, she was still a free agent and she would see whoever she wanted to see. But Jasmine clamped her lips shut, telling herself there was no point in discussing it now, not when he was in this kind of mood.

Yet she felt distinctly flat when he delivered her back to the apartment. His rugged features were still dark with rage as he bid her a terse farewell before striding out of the apartment without another word.

She stood in the empty sitting room after he'd gone, looking out as the golden sunlight bounced off the bright green of the treetops, realising how unsatisfactory the situation had become. She wanted him, yes—she had never stopped wanting him, if the truth were known—but for reasons of pride and self-preservation, she was no longer prepared to settle for what little he was prepared to offer her.

CHAPTER SIX

JASMINE FIRST REALISED something was wrong when she got a call to her mobile phone from an unlisted number. Deciding it was probably a sales call, she nonetheless picked it up, mainly because it had been ages since anyone had rung her.

'Hello?' she said cautiously.

'Is that Miss Jones? Miss Jasmine Jones?' The caller's voice was female, smoky and very confident.

'Speaking.'

'Just a couple of questions for you, Miss Jones. Is it true that you're the mother of the Sheikh of Razrastan's baby?'

Jasmine nearly dropped the phone. 'Who is this, please?'

'My name is Rebecca Starr from the *Daily View*,' said the voice. 'And I notice you're not issuing a denial to my question.'

Jasmine cut the connection with shaking fingers, wondering how the smoky-voiced Rebecca Starr had got hold of her number and wondering how best to respond. She swallowed. If in doubt, do nothing—wasn't that what people always said? She certainly wasn't going to bother Zuhal with it—not when he had stormed out in such a bad mood yesterday after that incident in the park with Carrie and her hot pants.

The phone rang again and Jasmine snatched it up, afraid that the shrill ringtone would wake her sleeping baby.

'Miss Jones? It's Rebecca Starr again. Do you have any immediate plans to marry Sheikh Zuhal Al Haidar of Razrastan?'

'Where did you get this number from?' Jasmine demanded uselessly.

'Because we understand there is a vacant role for a new royal Sheikha,' continued the journalist smoothly. 'Now that Zuhal is to be crowned King.'

With an angry squeak, Jasmine cut the connection, resisting the temptation to hurl the phone against one of the velvet cushions which were lined up neatly on the nearby sofa, knowing that if she did someone would just put them right back again. That was the trouble with having a fleet of cleaners at your disposal, she thought—there was never any mindless domestic work with which to displace your angry thoughts. No floors to clean or cobwebs to flick away from the ceiling.

She tried to convince herself that the press would soon lose interest if she didn't fan the flames of their story but she still felt faintly uneasy as she went about her normal routine. When he woke from his nap, she took Darius out for a stroll in his buggy and the warm sun beat down on the bare skin of her upper arms. Trying to ignore the discreet presence of the accompanying bodyguards, she found herself hoping she wouldn't bump into Carrie again, dreading having to bat away a stream of curious questions about Zuhal. But sooner or later she was going to have to see her, wasn't she? And what then? She couldn't pretend he didn't exist and she couldn't spend the rest of her life avoiding questions because she wasn't sure how to answer them.

She was just rounding the path to skirt the edge of the glittering lake when she sensed movement nearby and, glancing up, saw a blinding flash. Blinking, she watched as the black blur of one of the bodyguards hurtled towards a copse of trees while three others hurried forward to surround her.

'What's going on?' she questioned.

'Paparazzi,' one of them answered succinctly.

'What do they want?'

'Photos of you. And of the royal Prince. We need to leave, Miss Jones.'

'But—'

'Right now, Miss Jones,' he interrupted.

Jasmine forced herself to stay positive as she was practically marched back to the apartment—because having a baby meant you couldn't afford to indulge in introspective gloom—but she was glad when Rania stepped in to take Darius for her. And once she was on her own, reaction set in and Jasmine could do nothing to stop the jittery feelings which flooded over her. Her skin felt cold. Her hands were shaking and her heart was racing like a train. She wondered if this was how the future was going to look, with her locked away in her luxury apartment, hiding from anonymous people who took photos of her baby son without anyone's permission.

She wanted to pace the room. To talk to

someone, but mostly she wanted to talk to Zuhal—and that surprised her. Maybe it was because he was the only person who would understand. The only person who *could* understand, because Darius was his son too. She went into her bedroom—with its pristine bed and neatly folded nightdress on the pillow. The framed photos of Darius and the portrait study of her mother taken before disillusionment had set in were the sole signs that this room actually belonged to anyone. A single woman's bedroom, she thought, as she scrabbled around in one of the drawers for the phone number Zuhal had given her.

With fingers which were still shaking, she keyed in the numbers and Zuhal's almost instant pick-up brought her up with a start, because for some reason it hadn't occurred to her that he might give her his direct line. She pulled a face at her pale reflection in the mirror.

Did she really think so little of herself?

And why wouldn't she, when she had been cut so comprehensively from his life once before?

'Zuhal?'

'What's happening?' he demanded, his voice underpinned by something she'd never heard there before. 'Are you okay?'

'Yes. But I've been...been...' The words trembled on her lips and she found herself unable to say them.

'Ambushed by paparazzi?' he provided harshly.

She sucked in an audible breath. 'So your spies have already got back to you, have they?'

Amid the opulent surroundings of an aircraft which was more like a flying palace, Zuhal scowled. 'Of course they have,' he bit out. 'What do you think I pay my staff to do, Jazz? They are guarding my son. It's their duty to tell me exactly what's happening in his life at any given time and I gather someone was photographing you in the park.' Silently, he cursed the distance between them and her stubbornness in not having let him bring up Darius in a country where people would not have access to focus their long-range lens on an innocent little prince. And then he realised that she was ringing him and that was something new. Fear coursed through him in a way it had never done before. 'Has something else happened?' he demanded as dread rippled down his spine. 'Is Darius okay?'

'Darius is fine, but I...' He could hear her swallow. Could hear her try to piece her words together, even though her voice was shaking. 'I had a phone call from a journalist.'

He froze. 'Saying what?'

'Asking if I was the mother. Asking if...'

'If what, Jazz?'

He could hear the embarrassment in her voice. Or was it distaste? he wondered bitterly.

'If I was planning to marry you.'

Zuhal closed his eyes and allowed the prolonged silence to send its noiseless scream down the international phone line before hearing her cough.

'Zuhal? Are you still there?'

'Yes, I'm right here—but don't worry, I'll be with you very soon.'

'With me?' He could hear the confusion in her voice. 'But you told me you were going back to Razrastan.'

'I was,' he agreed grimly. 'But the moment I heard about the incident in the park, I had my jet made ready. I'm on my way back to London.'

'You're on your way back to London,' she repeated dully. 'And just what is that supposed to achieve?'

'I don't intend discussing it with you now, Jazz,' he snapped. 'I've always found the phone a particularly unsatisfactory form of communication.'

'Which is presumably why you avoided it in the past,' she said waspishly.

He scowled, but he wasn't going to get into an argument with her now. Especially not about things which had happened between them in the past. It was the future which needed addressing now, he thought grimly. 'Expect me in around three hours' time,' he said briefly, and cut the call.

Jasmine couldn't settle to anything as she waited for Zuhal to arrive. He didn't bother to ring the doorbell, he just let himself into the apartment—in a cruel parody of a husband returning home from work.

For a split second she almost didn't recognise him because for once he was wearing traditional robes and she'd only ever seen him dressed that way in photos. Her heart clenched in her chest and she felt a moment of aching awareness as she acknowledged his powerful and almost primitively alpha presence in the pristine apartment. His black hair was completely covered by a white silk headdress, knotted with a circlet of scarlet. The stark lines

made his hawkish profile appear more autocratic than usual, just as the flowing robes emphasised the hardness of his body, rather than
disguising it with its swishing folds. Maybe it
was because she was all too aware of what lay
beneath—all that muscular physique honed by
years of riding.

He flicked her an unfathomable look as
he strode towards the sitting room and what
choice did she have but to follow him? But Jasmine was aware of a new tension about him
and something indefinable glittering from his
black eyes.

'Is this what you wanted all along?' he queried silkily.

She blinked at him in confusion. 'What are
you talking about?'

'I'm talking about the sudden press interest,
which seems to have come out of nowhere.'

'And I'm supposed to have provoked it, is
that it?'

He shrugged. '*You* were the one who wanted
to walk in the park yesterday, remember?'

'Only because I was feeling positively claus-
trophobic stuck in here with you!'

His eyes grew hard. 'Did you set it all up
so that we'd bump into that woman Carrie—

who has clearly run straight to the newspapers about us?'

'How could I do that when I had no idea that you were going to take a walk with me?'

Zuhal sliced the condemnatory palm of his hand through the air. 'You could have phoned her when you were putting on your hat!'

'Well, I didn't!' she flared. 'I can't believe you'd think me even capable of such a thing— of putting my son at risk like that. How dare you?'

Zuhal was so taken aback by the fury in her voice that he let his hand fall to his side. And the crazy thing was that all he wanted to do was to kiss her—long and hard and deep. He wanted to take her in his arms and strip them both bare and lose all this anger and these recriminations. He scowled, because now was not the time to be distracted by the lure of sex, no matter how much he ached to be inside her again. The whole situation had got completely out of hand and it was now time for him to rein it all in, using the most effective means at his disposal.

He was going to have to do what he should have done the moment he found out about his son.

'You will have to come back to Razrastan with me,' he said.

'I beg your pardon?'

His mouth twisted. 'I don't think my statement requires any clarification.'

'You don't think your statement requires any clarification?' she repeated. 'Well, I do! What happened to keeping me here, with Darius as your insurance-policy heir, while you went out seeking a suitable bride?'

'I'll tell you exactly what happened,' he gritted out. 'My son has been discovered by the press. It hasn't hit the newspapers yet because my lawyers currently have an injunction out—but it will, because the courts will probably throw it out on the grounds that it's in the public interest to announce that Razrastan has a new heir. Even if they don't you can't keep something like this quiet for ever. Which is why the best kind of damage limitation is for you to agree to return to the guaranteed safety of my homeland.'

She shook her head. 'I can't do that, Zuhal,' she whispered.

Beneath his silken robes, Zuhal's body stiffened. Was she really refusing the gift he could offer her—a place of sanctuary while he worked out some kind of future for them all, even though he didn't yet know what that future could possibly be? She was a mass of contradictions, he conceded unwillingly—a woman who continually perplexed him. Who kept him at arm's length with a determination which was in itself a turn-on.

Yet he found himself remembering that moment in the park when he'd touched her and had seen her whole demeanour soften. Her green eyes had blazed with something passionate and unspoken. If that woman—Carrie—had not burst in on them, might he not have taken Jazz into his arms and kissed her? Brought her back here and spent the rest of the day having sex with her, so that once again she would become his compliant lover of old, eager to agree with whatever he suggested? When, instead, she was returning his gaze with a cool confidence which was making him seethe. So how best to proceed? He couldn't exactly drag her kicking and screaming back to Razrastan, could he? No matter how vivid *that* particular fantasy was turning out to be!

'You must realise that now I have discovered the existence of my son, nothing can ever be the same, Jazz.'

'You didn't discover him,' she answered. 'You came across him by chance.'

'However you care to define it,' he iced out, 'the facts remain the same. You are the mother of the Sheikh's son and you both remaining here in England is no longer a satisfactory option. You have no experience of press harassment but I do. You will be given no space until you provide them what they want, which is a story.'

She tipped her head back, her green eyes on a collision course with his. 'You really think I'd sell a story to the papers?'

'Actually, no. I don't.' He shook his head. 'But the story won't go away and in the meantime rumours will abound.'

'Rumours?' she questioned wryly. 'Or the truth?'

'The fact of our son is undeniable.' He gave a heavy sigh. 'I just need to figure out the best way to present it to my people and I can't do that if I'm constantly worried about you being besieged by all and sundry.'

'I don't know,' she hedged.

Sensing weakness, he swooped. 'Come back to Razrastan with me, Jazz,' he urged. 'Which will at least give us the space to think about the future.'

Jasmine turned away, touching her tongue to her dust-dry lips, her heart pounding as she acknowledged his words. He was promising nothing—certainly not on the emotional front. He'd spoken as if she were a plant he was eager to pluck from her native soil, to transplant her in his own, but with no assurances that she could thrive there. He wanted her to go to *his* palace and *his* country—where he literally ruled the roost. She would have absolutely no power there, and very little say in matters. And all this was complicated by her feelings for him, which wouldn't seem to go away. Because she still wanted him. Not just her body, but her heart, too. She wanted him in a way which was never going to happen and she knew that to go to his desert home would be to make herself vulnerable.

But what alternative did she have? Staying here and playing a constant cat-and-mouse game with the press? Continuing to obsess about him finding himself a suitable wife— a scenario which made her want to batter her fists against the walls of this elegant apartment which still didn't feel like home.

Would the royal palace feel any different? She bit her lip.

The chances were that it wouldn't but, for her son's sake, shouldn't she give it a *try*? To see if Zuhal's suggestion was in any way workable, even if she had no real faith in the idea?

'Very well,' she said slowly. 'I will bring Darius to Razrastan and we will consider our options.'

Zuhal nodded, but there was no sense of triumph or satisfaction in his heart at having won round one of what he suspected was going to be a difficult battle. Was he going to have to make Jazz his bride in order to get her to comply with his wishes?

His mouth hardened. She was not the kind of woman he had ever imagined marrying and he did not know if his people would accept her—but Razrastan required an heir, just as it required a king.

His country had never needed him before but it seemed that, suddenly, it did now.

CHAPTER SEVEN

ZUHAL WALKED INTO the lavishly appointed drawing room and suppressed a rising feeling of apprehension as he thought of what lay ahead. Forty-eight hours had passed since he'd arrived here in the palace, with the blonde Englishwoman and her son in tow. A child who was very obviously the fruit of his loins, although nobody had dared comment on that fact to his face. He'd been aware that his courtiers and staff were buzzing with questions they wouldn't dream of asking their ruler, but he also knew that sooner or later the subject would need to be addressed.

And this morning, he had done just that. He paced the room, the silk of his robes rippling over his bare flesh. His meeting with his closest advisors had concluded there was only one satisfactory way to provide the best possible future for his son.

Zuhal's throat constricted. His son. The small but sturdy scrap of humanity who bore his genes. He'd thought the disappearance of his elder brother had been the most seismic thing which could happen to him but he had been wrong. Becoming the unexpected ruler of this vast desert kingdom was certainly momentous but the thought of fatherhood was far more significant and he was still processing it.

His jaw tightened. During the flight here he had surreptitiously observed Darius during those moments when Jazz had been sleeping. Registering the coal-black curls and golden dark skin of the baby, he'd felt an unexpected thrill of accomplishment and pride shivering through his veins. He had managed to produce an heir to continue the powerful Al Haidar line, without even trying. And in that moment he had vowed that whatever happened between him and Jazz he would never allow her to remove Darius from the country he would one day rule.

Did she realise that?

He heard the sound of footsteps and looked up. Her footfall was soft on the marble floor and as he saw the pale gleam of her hair in the distance, he felt the instinctive jerk of his groin. He ran his gaze over her as she approached and found himself approving her unfamiliar appearance, thinking how perfect she looked in the part of would-be desert Queen. Surprisingly, she had made no resistance to the assortment of 'appropriate' clothes he had insisted on providing for her—as if recognising the need for the kind of high-specification wardrobe required of his fiancée. Her measurements had been dispatched to one of the palace couturiers and an array of soft silken robes in a muted spectrum of colours had been waiting on her arrival in the capital city of Dhamar. With a compliancy he hadn't been expecting, she had also approved the exquisite garments which had been procured for the infant Prince, despite her own ambitions in that particular area. In fact, the only things she'd brought with her from England were something called a baby monitor, which she had insisted on being installed as soon as they arrived, and a soft toy monkey, with bright eyes.

'Ah, Jazz,' he said, as she grew close and he could not help his gaze from drinking her in, as a thirsty man might drink after a long day in the desert. She was wearing a silky gown the colour of a ripe mango, which brought out the golden lights in her unusual eyes. He could see the luscious thrust of her breasts as their curved weight pushed against the fine material and he thought longingly of the way he used to trace patterns on them with his fingertips, before taking her nipple into his mouth and teasing it until she gasped aloud. He felt the rush of lust and it was with an effort that he dragged his eyes away to meet her gaze. 'I trust you've settled in well?' he questioned benignly. 'And that your quarters meet with your satisfaction.'

She gave a flicker of a smile. 'That's a bit of an understatement. They're absolutely amazing. I've never seen anything quite like them. Not even when I worked at the Granchester.'

Zuhal didn't like the implication that a hotel—no matter how grand—could possibly be compared to his royal palace, but he made no comment. She would soon learn what were and were not acceptable topics of conversation, but now was not the time for a short lesson in diplomacy! He inclined his head. 'I'm glad you think so,' he said. 'And now, we will feast. I trust you have some appetite tonight, Jazz—for the servants inform me that you have eaten remarkably little since our arrival.'

She raised her eyebrows. 'Does that mean I'm still being spied on—despite living in your palace with practically no contact with the outside world?'

'I prefer to think of it as looking out for your welfare,' he corrected spikily. 'So why don't you sit down over there?'

The sweeping movement of his hand indicated an ornate table which had been laid up in one of the recessed windows overlooking the floodlit rose garden. On golden platters were elaborate displays of glistening fruits and savoury dishes, as well as tall decanters of iced fruit juice. Since he'd dispensed with all his servants, it meant Zuhal now found himself in the highly unusual position of having to serve her with food and drinks himself. And he thought she seemed completely oblivious to the honour he was affording her.

'Thank you,' she replied, perching on one of the gilt-edged chairs, before accepting the glass he was offering. 'Mmm… Delicious,' she added, as she sipped at the iced pomegranate juice.

He sat down opposite her and spooned some stewed aubergine onto her plate. 'How is Darius settling in?' he questioned.

'Better than I thought he would,' she said, as she lifted up her fork. 'Even the change in climate and the fact that we've leapt ahead by a few hours doesn't seem to have perturbed him. He's just had his bath and I've read him a story and now he's fast asleep. He won't wake until morning.'

'How can you be so certain?'

'Because that's his routine.' She hesitated for a moment, as if gauging his interest was genuine, before forging on. 'It's a routine I deliberately established, because I knew I'd never get time to get any sewing done otherwise. He's broken it a few times of course and once, when he was running a temperature, he was awake all night long.'

'And what was that like?' he questioned, his curiosity aroused.

'It was a nightmare,' she admitted. 'He screamed from dusk to daybreak. It was...' she gave a rather helpless shrug '...a long night.'

'I'm sure it was.' He realised with a start how much she'd had to deal with. That, despite

Darius being an easy child, there had been
nobody else for her to turn to—and surely
that must have been hard, to have done it all
on her own. Unexpectedly, he felt the stir of
his conscience and suddenly he found himself wanting her to relax. To lose that pinched
look which was making her face seem so pale.
To become more like the Jazz of old, rather
than this new, wary version. With this aim in
mind, he coaxed her with food and watched
as she tried a thimble-sized glass of Razrastan's famous lychee dessert wine, and it was
with pleasure that he saw some of the tension
leave her. 'Is there anything else you require?'
he questioned solicitously. 'Anything my staff
can help you with?'

Jasmine tried to concentrate on his question, but it wasn't easy. All she could think
about was how frustrating it was to be within
touching distance, when they hadn't actually
touched at all. And while she knew this was
probably the most *sensible* outcome—it certainly wasn't what her body wanted.

She couldn't seem to stop staring at his olive-dark face, wishing she could tug off that
cream headdress and tangle her fingers in the
rich blackness of his hair. She could feel her

breasts tightening beneath her robe and the insistent tug of desire low in her belly as she surreptitiously ran her gaze over him. Suddenly it seemed like an awfully long time since she'd had sex. Well, it was. Over eighteen months, to be precise—and increasing exposure to the father of her child was reminding her all too vividly that she was a healthy young woman with physical needs of her own.

She found herself wanting to touch him— just as she had done when he had unexpectedly reappeared in her life again and had kissed her so passionately in her run-down little Oxford cottage. Maybe even more, because being with him again reminded her just how much she had always fancied him. And it wasn't his royal status which set her heart racing, or the fact that he was one of the wealthiest men on the planet. To her he was the man who had awoken her sexuality— the only man she had given her heart and her body to—and a woman never forgot something like that.

This was the man who used to flutter soft kisses over her belly before licking his tongue between the eager parting of her thighs. Who had brought her to orgasm that way, his hungry lips drinking in every shuddered spasm she made. The first time he'd done that she'd been incredibly nervous—self-conscious, even. But Zuhal had taught her that sex was a gift to be enjoyed and there should be no barriers between consenting lovers. He had known her body inside and out, and sometimes, when he'd been deep inside her, it had been difficult to know where he began and she ended.

But she hadn't been thinking about that when she'd reluctantly agreed to come to Razrastan. She'd been thinking about her son. And now all her guilt about Darius not having had a father figure had been replaced by the fear that she'd walked into some sort of gilded trap. From the moment she'd entered the palace, the glittering walls seemed to enclose her with all their heavily guarded splendour. She'd looked around the vast and ornate citadel, slightly dazed to realise that Zuhal owned everything as far as the eye could see.

But he didn't own her, and that was what she needed to remember.

He had brought her and Darius here to get them away from a curious press and work out some kind of plan for the future—even though he had given her no indication of what that plan might be. He'd made it clear about the kind of woman he expected to marry and it certainly wasn't her—not that she'd want to marry such a cold-hearted brute in any case. Surely he wasn't expecting her to stay here indefinitely, while they lived separate lives?

She sighed, knowing she was going to have to make an effort. She needed to get on with the father of her child, no matter what happened between the two of them. So she nodded in response to Zuhal's unusually solicitous questions. 'There's nothing more we need,' she told him. 'Our rooms couldn't be any more comfortable and the view over the palace gardens is breathtaking. I had no idea that you could grow so many flowers in such a hot climate.'

'Fortunately, we do have access to water,' he commented sardonically, a dismissive wave of his hand indicating he was done with horticultural small-talk. 'And what of the nursemaids who will assist Rania? I trust they also meet with your approval, Jazz.'

It was a statement rather than a question and Jasmine hesitated, recognising once again that negotiation was better than confrontation.

'I have no complaints,' she said. 'They seem very…capable.'

'They are,' he agreed. 'Like Rania, many of them are the daughters of the women who used to care for Kamal and I when we were young.'

Jasmine nodded, his words reminding her that his upbringing was a million miles away from hers—a young prince surrounded by an army of servants. She realised she'd hardly ever heard him mention his own mother, not even when they'd been at their most intimate—actually, he'd barely mentioned his early years and neither had she. But back then their focus had been solely on pleasure, rather than the exchange of confidences which might have brought them closer as a couple. She met the black burn of his eyes. 'I wanted to talk to you about that,' she said hesitantly. 'You know, there's no need for a nurse to sit in the same room, watching Darius while he sleeps. I'm sure Rania and I can manage perfectly well on our own.'

'But I want something more for my son than just *managing*,' he bit out. 'Darius will one day be King, and will need to get used to the presence of servants.'

Jasmine narrowed her eyes. 'You can't just come out and say things like that,' she objected, all thoughts of compromise forgotten. 'He might want to be a bank manager, living in the English countryside.'

He shook his head. 'No, not that. Not ever that. He will be King of Razrastan.'

'And how is that ever going to happen?' she demanded baldly.

His lips twisted into an odd kind of smile. 'I think you know the answer to that, Jazz,' he said softly. 'Darius will be my legitimate heir—and in order for that to happen, you must become my wife.'

A brittle silence entered the atmosphere as Jasmine stared at Zuhal with disbelieving eyes. 'Become your wife?' she repeated faintly.

'Surely the idea doesn't come as a complete shock to you?' he suggested sardonically. 'I have spoken with my closest advisors and government this very morning. They think my people will accept you, since you are the mother of my son. And, if the subject is handled with delicacy and tact, see no reason why we shouldn't marry. In fact, they concluded that marriage is the only appropriate solution to this particular dilemma.'

'*Dilemma?*' she echoed, outrage beginning to bubble up inside her. 'Is that how you see me?'

'Please don't fixate on the words I'm using but think instead about the meaning of what I'm saying, Jazz,' he continued remorselessly. 'I am proposing marriage. I, the Sheikh, am asking you, the commoner, to be my bride. Don't you realise what a great compliment that is?'

Jasmine shook her head. It didn't feel like a compliment. It felt like…

As if Zuhal was being forced into doing something he didn't want to do. As if he had been backed into a corner with no other way out. And wasn't that the truth of it? He didn't love her. He'd never loved her—so what were the chances of having a successful marriage? She thought about her own parents. About her mother's reaction when the relationship had started to crumble and the desperate way she'd tried to cling on. *I don't want to become like my mother,* Jasmine thought suddenly. And I don't want an uncaring sheikh's power to diminish me as a person, just because he wants to claim Darius as his rightful heir.

'It's too early to talk about marriage,' she

said, quickly getting up from the table, unwilling to be subjected to Zuhal's look of disbelief as she gave him her answer. Resolutely, she walked over to one of the huge windows, glancing up at an indigo sky and thinking how far away the spatter of silver stars looked. 'Way too early.'

'Your attitude is more than a little *insulting*, Jazz,' he said, and she could hear the scrape of his chair and the sound of his footsteps as he walked over to join her. 'Don't you realise that most women would be eager to become my Queen?'

He was standing beside her—so close that they were almost touching. The warmth of his body was almost palpable and his presence was so powerful that Jasmine could scarcely breathe as raw longing clogged in her throat. 'Maybe they don't know you as well as I do!' She turned her head to look at him, detecting a brief flicker of outrage in the inky blaze of his eyes. 'I think we should take things slowly. I think, right now, that caution is probably the wisest choice.'

He gave a low laugh, which trickled over her skin like warm honey. 'Forgive me if I disagree,' he murmured, 'but I think a little recklessness might work better in our favour.'

She saw something in his eyes which was achingly familiar, as was the sudden tension which entered his hard body. And then suddenly Jasmine was in his arms and she never knew which of them instigated it, only that it seemed as inevitable as the rising of the giant moon outside the window, which was bathing them with a strange, silvery light. The Sheikh's mouth hovered briefly over hers and Jasmine gave a yelp as he brought it down hard to kiss her—before kissing him back with an urgent hunger which seemed to make her world spin. It felt as if she were falling. Or drowning. Drowning in a sweet, molten tide of desire.

Last time he'd kissed her, she'd felt a certain amount of restraint for all kinds of reasons, but mainly because she'd been concealing the knowledge of her son. Now she was concealing nothing. Not a single thing. She felt naked—despite the flowing material of the robes which covered her. She could feel the shameless spring of his erection pushing hard against her belly and felt the corresponding opening of her thighs as if she were silently girding herself to accommodate him. She heard his soft laugh as he acknowledged her submission, and his arms tightened around her back.

And Jasmine hugged him back because, oh, how she wanted this.

Now.

Here.

Just like this.

The real world retreated and all that mattered was the incredible sensation Zuhal was provoking by the tantalising whisper of a fingertip which traced its way down her spine. It was a gesture which felt almost innocent, yet how could it possibly be innocent when her nipples were hardening into tight buds which felt as if they were about to explode? He gave a low laugh of pleasure as he tilted her chin so that she was dazzled by the close-up fire of his eyes.

'Oh, Jazz,' he said softly. 'You want me, don't you? You want me so much, baby. You always did.'

His mocking smile dared her to deny it, but how could she deny it when it was the truth? When she'd dreamed and fantasised about this in weak moments when her defences had been down. Gazing up into the hectic gleam of his eyes, Jasmine was aware of her almost imperceptible nod of consent and the Sheikh's low growl of pleasure before he bent his dark head to kiss her again.

CHAPTER EIGHT

HIS HUNGRY HANDS were on her breasts, her bottom and her belly as sexual heat ripped through Jasmine like a desert storm. Zuhal's fingers were moving urgently over her as if he couldn't wait to reacquaint himself with every inch of quivering flesh. She clung to his shoulders for support as he pulled her closer with a possessive mastery which made her feel weak with desire.

'Zuhal,' she breathed, the warmth of her breath mingling eagerly with his, the heat in her lower body starting its restless throb.

He didn't reply. Not at first. His only response was to deepen the kiss—his tongue exploring her with breathtaking intimacy. Her heart was racing like a piston as her fingers touched the unfamiliar headdress and she gave an impatient little tug to remove it. It slithered redundantly to the marble floor and suddenly his head was bare, just like in the old days. Exultantly, her fingertips explored the thick silk of his hair, before kneading at the base of his neck in a way which made him give an instinctive murmur of appreciation. Her hands moved to his biceps—powerful and supremely strong beneath his desert robes. She began to massage the rippling flesh and felt a familiar tension enter his body as he circled his hips in a way which made her intensely aware of his erection.

Jasmine closed her eyes as she felt that steely column pressing into her belly, suddenly aware of everything which had happened since they'd last made love. She recognised that her body had done some amazing things during that time. It had grown and given birth to a baby—an accomplishment which seemed both unreal and marvellous. But this was different. This was hunger. Sexual hunger. A raw and primitive need which was fierce and all-consuming. It was eating her up from the inside and igniting a yearning so powerful that she felt almost unable to stand.

Did Zuhal realise that? Was that why he drew back and stared down at her for a long moment—his eyes glittering like polished jet—before scooping her up into his arms with a moan which called out to her aching heart? When for a moment he seemed like the embodiment of all things alpha as he towered over her, dark and strong and vital as he carried her across the shiny marble floor towards an arched entrance at the far end of the vast chamber, his robes flowing like liquid silk as he walked.

'Where are we going?' she gasped, as he dipped his head to enter a narrow corridor, whose ceiling gleamed with exquisite inlaid tiles depicting erotic scenes of cavorting lovers.

'Somewhere where we'll be more comfortable.'

She looked up into the hectic gleam of his black eyes. 'Somewhere?'

'My bedroom,' he clarified unsteadily. 'It is connected to your apartments through this passageway, which is unseen by anyone else and which only the King is permitted to use. But I grant you my permission to use it any time you wish, Jazz.'

They emerged into a room which was way more magnificent than the suite which had been assigned to her and Darius, but for once

Jasmine wasn't daunted by the size or splendour of the accommodation. Exquisite furniture and several statues swam in and out of focus, but all she could see was the vast bed, which Zuhal was striding towards.

Dimly she became aware of him impatiently brushing aside a litter of cushions before laying her down on it, his black gaze raking over her with a look of hungry speculation. Her hands were lying above her head and her legs were splayed out beneath the soft silken robes. And in that moment she felt like a sacrifice about to be offered up to the gods—a feeling which should surely have repelled the modern woman she was—yet the expression on his face spoke to some deep need inside her and she knew there was no power on earth which could have made her resist him.

'Oh, Jazz,' he groaned as he lay down beside her, his lips at her neck, his practised hand already rucking up the slippery fabric of her gown as his mouth drifted to her ear. 'You look so beautiful lying there.'

'D-do I?'

'Utterly.' he husked. 'Do you know how much I want you?'

'I think…' She closed her eyes as he began

to drift kisses over her neck. 'I think I can just about work it out.'

'Then double it,' he growled. 'Better still, triple it.'

His hungry words thrilled her—they made her heart race even harder. She remembered the first time he'd taken her to bed, when her heart had swelled up with so much joy. When she'd cried—she wasn't quite sure why—when he had taken her virginity, and he had dried away her tears with a touch which had seemed almost tender.

And although some tiny voice in her head was telling her this was different—was urging her to employ caution—Jasmine refused to listen. Because how could she possibly be cautious when Zuhal's fingers were at her breasts? When they were cupping each swollen mound so that the mango silk appeared bright against his burnished flesh. And now his hand was inching its way up her leg, his featherlight fingertips brushing against the silky flesh of her inner thigh so that goosebumps were flowering beneath his touch. She could feel a syrupy rush soaking her panties and Jasmine closed her eyes before opening them again. 'Zuhal,' she said weakly, and just saying his name out loud was making her even more excited.

'Do you like that?'

'You...you know I do,' she managed to say, but only just—because now he had reached her panties and his finger was tracing a teasing path over the delicate fabric, which stretched tightly over her aching mound. Jasmine swallowed. How could she have forgotten that her body could ever feel like *this*?

'And this?' he questioned, almost carelessly.

She almost shot off the bed as skilfully he targeted her quivering clitoris. 'Oh, yes,' she groaned. '*Yes.*'

'How much do you like it?' he murmured.

'A...a lot,' she breathed.

'Then let's see if we can do something you like even more, shall we? Any ideas, Jazz?'

'I'll... I'll leave those to you,' she gasped. 'You were always the one with the ideas.'

Pushing aside the damp fabric, he began to thrum his finger against her moist flesh and Jazz began to quiver as his hand took on that slick rhythm she hadn't felt for so long. Already she felt crazily close to coming, knowing that if she let him continue she would succumb to the intense orgasm which was building up inside her. And wasn't that what she wanted? Wasn't that *all* she wanted? A quick, physical release to satisfy her aching body—with no danger of compromising her heart. Fractionally she lifted her hips and squirmed, her silent invitation to continue with his ministrations all too obvious. But Zuhal obviously had other ideas. Pulling his hand away and allowing it to rest indolently against the springy curls of her pubic hair, he pressed his lips into her ear.

'No,' he breathed hotly. 'Not like that. Not the first time. I want to feel myself inside you again, Jazz. Deep inside you, where I belong.'

His erotic words rocked her. They set up an answering clamour in her body which made her long to accommodate him. But even as her trembling thighs were spreading open to welcome him, that cautious voice of earlier was louder now, and less easy to ignore. It was reminding her that his words weren't true. That this wasn't the *first time*. Far from it. She was countless episodes and almost two years away from that initial deflowering, which had taken him by surprise. She was no longer the virgin divorcee he had rapturously introduced to sex. Nor was she the idealistic innocent who believed that just because a man groaned out heartfelt words of desire when he was orgasming inside you, it meant any more than just physical satisfaction. With Zuhal it had only *ever* been about physical satisfaction. But now there was something else he wanted even more badly. His baby son. Was that what this was all about? Softening her with seduction while he plotted to take what he saw as rightfully his?

Did he think that if she had sex with him now she would instantly agree to marriage?

Because that had been part of the trouble before—she'd allowed passion to sweep her away, so that she wasn't really thinking straight. Was that why she had tolerated her very part-time role as his mistress and been content to live in the shadows of his life? Maybe that was what amazing sex did to you… it robbed you of your strength and logic—and she needed both those things like never before. For her son's sake, but also for her own.

Her thoughts blurred as he slipped a finger inside her panties and she knew that if she didn't stop him soon, she would be past the point of making a rational decision…

Wriggling free of his intimate caress, she somehow managed to scramble off the day-bed, steeling herself against the sight of Zuhal still lying there in his rumpled robes, two high lines of colour flushed across his autocratic cheekbones, his black eyes burning with an expression she couldn't quite work out.

'Was it something I said?' he questioned mockingly.

Flattening her fingers against her heaving breasts, Jasmine struggled to get her breath back. 'That...that wasn't supposed to happen!'

'No?' He raised his black brows. 'So just what did you *think* was going to happen when I carried you in here, Jazz? Did you think we were going to have a discussion about world politics, or that I was about to start regaling you with stories of Razrastanian history?'

She realised that although outwardly he appeared cool and in control, his sarcastic words were underpinned with unmistakable irritation as he folded his arms behind his head to cushion it. She couldn't blame him.

'I'm sorry.' Distractedly, she shook her head. 'I wasn't thinking.'

There was a pause as his black eyes bored into her. 'Why don't you want to have sex with me, Jazz?'

She could feel the burn of her cheeks. She

shouldn't have allowed him to bring her in here, putting herself in a situation she couldn't handle. Because wasn't the truth that she wanted to go right back over there and have him touch her with all that sweet unerring accuracy again? Didn't she long to feel him inside her—*deep inside her*—as he himself had groaned out a few minutes ago?

But a few moments of pleasure weren't powerful enough to make her forget why she was here. He'd offered her marriage but she was still unsure of what her answer was going to be. Because surely she could only accept if she felt equipped enough to cope with a loveless union. The last thing she needed was to be blinded by desire. 'Because sex will just complicate things. Surely you can see that.'

'You're saying you don't want us to be intimate?' he queried softly.

Her voice was stiff as she tried to give an honest answer. 'I'd be a liar if I said I didn't want it. I just…just don't feel ready for it at the moment.'

'Maybe that's something you ought to think about next time you start batting those big green eyes at me,' he observed, a little pulse hammering frantically at his temple.

She gave an awkward nod of acknowledgement. 'We were both responsible for what just happened, not just me. We got…carried away.'

'And then some,' he agreed drily.

Attempting to put some space between them, Jasmine walked across the room to stand beside a marble statue of a winged creature which was half-falcon, half-goat— before turning back to face him. But he was still tempting her. She suspected that he always would. 'I'll try to be more circumspect in future,' she said.

There was a pause. 'Even if that means resisting your own desires?'

She met the curious question gleaming in the depths of his ebony eyes. Could she explain what was making her so cautious, without coming over as vulnerable or needy in the process? 'Here in your lavish palace, the only thing I have is my integrity and I don't intend to compromise it,' she said. 'I won't be able to think straight if we become intimate again. I'm afraid that desire will cloud my judgement and I can't afford to let that happen.'

'These are fighting words, Jazz,' he observed softly.

'They aren't meant to be. I don't want to

fight with you, Zuhal.' She drew in a deep breath, praying her new-found conviction wouldn't leave her. Praying she wouldn't morph back into that docile Jasmine of old who had been content with the crumbs of affection the powerful Sheikh had thrown her way. 'We're no longer two occasional lovers who can't keep their hands off each other. We're parents. We have a lifetime bond through our son. We rushed into a relationship once before without really getting to know one another. This time, I think we should take things more slowly—to decide whether or not we could make a marriage work.'

'And am I supposed to admire your reluctance?' he questioned. 'Is your elusiveness part of some complex female game of playing hard to get in order to make yourself seem more of a prize?'

'I can assure you I'm not playing games, Zuhal. This is much too important for that. I have to believe that there's a basic compatibility between us before I agree to become your wife—otherwise it's just a recipe for disaster.'

Zuhal shook his head, unable to believe that Jazz of all people was turning him down. A woman who had been eager to learn all he could teach her—who had been the most delightful of all his lovers. Was she holding out for what women always demanded—words of love he would not provide? *Could* not provide, he reminded himself bitterly. If Jasmine wanted violins and moonlight she was doomed to be disappointed.

He looked at her. During that tantalising tumble which had just taken place on his bed, her hair had come free from its ribbon and was now tumbling down in waves of golden silk. She looked like an angel, he thought reluctantly, her long lashes shuttering the verdant beauty of her green eyes. He watched her smoothing down her robes as she struggled to catch her breath and in that moment she looked like the Jasmine he remembered— young and wild and passionate. But this Jasmine had just pushed him away in a way she would never have done before.

For a moment he was tempted to walk over there and attempt to change her mind. Would she have the strength to resist him a second time? He suspected not as for a moment he imagined being inside her again, his length encased inside her molten tightness as he rocked them both towards that blissful goal.

But he wasn't going to do that. She would regret soon enough having turned him down and discover that he had no intention of chasing after her all the way to the altar. Did she really think a man in his position would ever have to grovel to a woman? His lips hardened into a smile.

Let her come to him.

'So what exactly is it you want of me, Jazz?' he enquired casually.

It was a question Jasmine had never thought he'd ask. She knew what she'd wanted when they'd been together before but had accepted she was never going to get it. Because you couldn't demand love when instinct told you that love was an alien concept to a man like Zuhal. But she could discover more about the man who had always been a closed book to her when they had been casual lovers, couldn't she?

'Obviously, I'd like to learn about your country and your culture, Zuhal. But I'd also like to learn more about you.'

'Even though you've just turned down a method guaranteed to do exactly that?'

'I didn't find out much about you in all the time we were together, did I? And we were having plenty of sex back then.'

He raised his eyebrows. 'There are official biographies you can look at,' he said coolly. 'Which have always been in the public domain. We even have the authorised versions here in the palace library, which you are perfectly at liberty to read.'

She shook her head. 'That's not what I meant.'

'Oh?'

It was the most forbidding of looks and maybe if so much hadn't been at stake, Jasmine might have heeded its silent warning. But there was a potential marriage to consider, and it had to have the makings of a good one for her to risk putting Darius at its centre. And how could she consider marrying a man who remained little more than a stranger?

'I want to hear it from you, Zuhal,' she said. 'From your lips, not somebody else's.'

She saw his face darken with frustration, irritation and then a grim kind of acceptance. 'Very well,' he said at last, bending to pick up the discarded headdress which she had pulled from his head. 'You'd better speak to my diary secretary.'

'Your diary secretary?' she echoed in confusion.

'Of course.' He gave the flicker of a smile edged with undeniable *triumph*. 'How else did you think I was going to find time to see you? I am King now, with many demands on my time. Speaking of which…' he glanced at his watch '… I must leave you now, since I have work to do.'

She blinked. 'What, now?'

His black eyes glittered. 'There is always work to do, Jazz, no matter what the clock says. And since the evening has fallen far short of my expectations, I might as well put what remains of it to good use. I will show you back to your rooms and anything you require, just ring and one of the servants will attend to you.'

A peremptory wave of his hand indicated she should precede him. But it did more than that—it made it very clear who was in charge.

Jasmine opened her mouth to object before shutting it again, because what could she say? She had turned down his proposal and now he was suggesting she make an appointment to see him, in the same way he might schedule in an appointment with his dentist! And meanwhile that vast and rumpled bed was mocking her with all its unused promise.

The bubble of the evening seemed to have burst. She walked ahead of him, hearing the soft shimmer of his robes brushing over the marble floor as he followed her. And all she could think about was the powerful perfection of his brooding body and the way it had felt when he'd held her in his arms again, as she tried to quash a deep and overwhelming sense of regret.

CHAPTER NINE

IT SHOULD HAVE been a fairy tale. At least, that was how it might have looked to an outsider. A one-time single mother plucked from her humble abode and transplanted into a glittering, golden palace by a sheikh who was eager for her to be his bride.

A lump rose in Jasmine's throat. Because this was no fairy tale. This was living in a gilded prison.

It was true she'd been meeting all kinds of new people—from royal monarchs who ruled neighbouring countries to the noblemen and women of Razrastan itself. She'd sat beneath sparkling chandeliers, wearing a fortune in diamonds around her neck—while discussing with the American ambassador the proposed trip by the President of the United States of America!

Those were the facts.

The irrefutable facts.

But facts only told you so much. They only showed you the supposedly smooth surface— not the dark undercurrents which were swirling beneath. She might be the mother of the Sheikh's baby, and they might be polite and perfectly civil with each other in public. But in reality they'd barely spent any time alone since she had rejected Zuhal's sexual advances, and the subject of marriage was still unresolved.

She'd wanted to get to know him before making any firm commitment, but how was that possible when palace life seemed the enemy of intimacy? When meals were distinctly formal and featured guests Zuhal thought it prudent she meet. During course after endless course, streams of servants weaved their way in and out, bearing extravagant dishes heaped with Razrastanian specialities, whose very names dazzled her. None of the servants ever met her eyes. They seemed to look right through her. She suspected they disapproved of this Englishwoman who had entered their royal palace with an illegitimate baby in tow. Maybe they were glad there had been no official acknowledgement of her role in the Sheikh's life.

And none of these functions offered any opportunity for private conversation with Zuhal because he was always sitting at the far end of the table, looking impossibly aloof and regal. Why, the physical distance between them was so great, that just getting him to hear her meant she almost had to shout. Just as there had been no shared moments of parenting with him. It seemed he made time to see his son only when he was certain Jasmine wasn't around and she wondered if he was punishing her for refusing his proposal, by deliberately keeping his distance. On more than one occasion, she had emerged from her dressing room, her hair still damp from the shower, to see the silky shimmer of the Sheikh's pale robes disappearing through the tall, arched doorway.

Sometimes she would wake early when the baby was still asleep and the palace all but silent. Once, unable to get back to sleep, she had gone to the stable complex, just as Zuhal was dismounting from his horse after his morning ride. Hidden away in the shadows, he hadn't seen her, but Jasmine had watched as he'd peeled a silk shirt from his torso. Like a woman hypnotised, she had observed his slow striptease with a racing heart which had threatened to burst out of her chest. With hungry eyes she'd drunk in the gleam of his burnished skin and bronzed definition of his powerful physique. There wasn't an inch of surplus flesh on his hard body and his washboard abs were glistening like the cover shot of a fitness magazine. She'd found herself wanting to run over and to slowly slide her way down over his body. To lick her tongue over his chest, revelling in the taste of each salty bead of sweat, knowing they were all a part of him. And then to unzip his jodhpurs and feel his proud length springing free, first against her fingers and then into the moist and waiting cavern of her lips.

She began to question if she'd been too hasty. If she had driven him away with her proud stance, which had masked her fears about getting intimate with him again. Yet how was she ever going to find out whether they were compatible if they were never alone? When the days were ticking away, bringing closer the formal signing of the papers which would make Zuhal the official ruler of Razrastan. She hadn't actually ruled out marriage, had she? She'd just told him she wanted to get to know him better before she committed. So maybe it was time for action instead of all these fractured thoughts. Maybe she should take Zuhal at his word and book herself an appointment to see him, since he obviously had no intention of backing down himself.

Which was how one sun-dappled morning she found herself in Zuhal's offices in the south-west corner of the palace, which overlooked a sylvan courtyard of trees. At its centre was a cool pond, in which red-gold fish swam—giving the place a curiously peaceful feel. Inside, it was completely different—a modern hive of activity hiding behind the ancient doors. Assistants tapped feverishly at the keyboards of sleek computers and rows of clocks indicated different time zones from around the world. She was asked to wait in an anteroom, before being shown into an inner sanctum for a meeting with Zuhal's chief aide—a shuttered-faced man in traditional Razrastanian robes, who looked up from his desk as she was ushered in.

'Miss Jones,' he said smoothly, rising to his feet to greet her. 'My name is Adham. This is an unexpected pleasure.'

Jasmine recognised his voice instantly. She would never forget it, not in a million years.

A chill rippled down her spine. This was the same aide who had blocked her attempt to tell Zuhal she was pregnant all those months ago. Was that why his face was so unfriendly when he looked at her? Why she detected a glimmer of darkness in his expression as she entered his plush office? Or was he just more open about expressing what she suspected most of the palace staff really felt about her? Quashing down her instinctive apprehension, Jasmine composed her face into a look of polite enquiry. 'I hope I'm not disturbing you?'

'Not at all, Miss Jones,' he said, his forced smile seeming to contradict his benign words. 'What can I do for you this morning?'

Jasmine felt the sudden pounding of her heart, recognising that this was the moment. She was here to try to deepen her relationship with the father of her child and to address seriously the possibility of being a future queen. So maybe it was time to start acting like one. To show Adham that she was no longer some inconvenient lover he could dismiss as if she didn't matter, but part of Zuhal's life, whether he liked it or not.

Adopting the wide smile which had always been super-effective when dealing with tricky customers at the Granchester boutique, she gestured towards the sunlit garden outside. 'It is an exceptionally beautiful morning, isn't it?' she observed, with diplomatic politeness.

'Indeed. The weather in Razrastan is especially temperate at this time of year,' Adham answered, the faint elevation of his eyebrows silently urging her to get to the point.

Jasmine did exactly that. 'I'd like to see the Sheikh, please.'

'I'm afraid that won't be possible, Miss Jones. His Royal Highness is busy at the moment. I'm sure you are well aware of the demands on his time at this key stage in the country's future,' he said, his tone smooth and pleasant, although the icy gleam of his eyes suggested a certain insincerity. 'In fact, he is on the phone to the Sheikh of Maraban, as we speak.'

'Oh, I didn't mean *right now*,' said Jasmine quickly. 'Obviously, he's tied up most of the time. I appreciate that. I just wondered if you could make an appointment for me to see him.'

A flicker of incredulity passed over the shuttered features. 'An appointment, Miss Jones?'

'If you would. Zuhal did say we should coordinate our diaries in order to make time for one other.'

'His Royal Highness mentioned nothing to me.'

'Does Zuhal run everything past you, then, Adham?' questioned Jasmine innocently.

It was the first time in her life that she'd ever pulled rank—not that she'd ever had any rank to pull before now—and to her astonishment it worked. As if realising that this time she wouldn't be thwarted, the aide reluctantly bent his head to study the leatherbound diary in front of him before returning his shuttered gaze to hers. 'Very well. I believe I can fit you in, if you are prepared to be flexible. Shall we say tomorrow morning at ten o'clock? His Royal Highness has a window of thirty minutes he can allot to you, after his morning ride.'

Thirty minutes! Not even an hour alone with the man who had asked her to marry him! And just around the time when Darius would be having his post-breakfast playtime, which wasn't what you'd call convenient. But if this was the best she could hope for, then she was going to grab it with both hands. 'Perfect,' she said brightly.

The aide consulted some sort of grid chart in front of him. 'If you would like to make your way to the Damask Room at the allotted time, His Royal Highness will join you there.

Jasmine nodded. 'Thank you, Adham.'

Despite the somewhat lukewarm response she'd received, Jasmine felt a fizz of excitement as she returned to her suite, where Darius was waiting with Rania. The baby gurgled with pleasure as she held out her arms to him and her mind was buzzing as she wondered how to make the most of her time alone with Zuhal tomorrow.

Was that being super-needy?

No, she told herself, as she waved a noisy rattle in front of the baby's nose. Not needy at all. It was being grown-up and sensible. Accepting that she wasn't dealing with just *any* man. She closed her eyes with pleasure as Darius wrapped his chubby little arms around her neck and snuggled up close. Zuhal was a man who would soon be King and she needed to make allowances for that.

But that night, during a pre-dinner drinks reception for a cluster of visiting Argentinean diplomats, she looked up to find the Sheikh's eyes fixed on hers more often than usual. The expression in their ebony depths was one she couldn't decipher, but it was enough to set her heart racing as she walked forward to meet the line of guests.

She had decided to treat these functions in the same way she used to regard shopping evenings at the Granchester boutique, trying to put people at their ease—and for the most part this made them bearable. Yet tonight it felt different. Or maybe it was just she who felt different. She'd broken the deadlock and from tomorrow, she would start learning more about the Sheikh whose narrowed gaze was currently sweeping over her like a dark spotlight. She wished he wouldn't look at her like that in public. Making her dress feel as if it had suddenly become two sizes too small. Making her brow break out into tiny little beads of sweat beneath her carefully coiffed hair.

As usual, she and Zuhal left the reception at exactly the same time but tonight, instead of going to his own suite, he insisted on accompanying her to Darius's room where he remained while she checked on him, before dismissing Rania for the night. The main reception room of her private suite seemed very large and echoing as she shut the door to the nursery and turned to Zuhal, realising that, for the first time in a long time, they were completely alone. She swallowed. She could detect the subtle yet very masculine scent of sandalwood radiating from his powerful body, making her uncomfortably aware of his raw virility as she regarded him with cautious question in her eyes.

'I understand you paid a visit to Adham this morning,' he said, without prompting.

'I did.'

'And insisted on a meeting with me tomorrow morning.'

Wasn't his expression more than a little *smug*? Jasmine wondered, with a touch of indignation. 'Insist?' she echoed lightly. 'I thought that's what we agreed. Appointments in the diary. A rather unconventional way of a couple getting to know each other, it's true, but that was the only way you could guarantee allotting me any time.'

'It's true, that's what we agreed,' Zuhal conceded, feasting his gaze on her luscious body and letting it linger there. He'd said it to make her realise that he had neither the time nor the inclination to play games with her. He'd imagined his cool indifference might make her reconsider her foolishness in rejecting him and bring her running into his arms. That without further prompting she would slip along the secret corridor to his bed and seek the pleasure she was guaranteed to find there.

But it hadn't worked out that way.

His remoteness hadn't had the desired effect of taming her or bringing her into his bed. There had been no delicious blonde lying waiting for him between the slippery silk of his sheets, eagerly taking him into her arms before spreading those delicious thighs for him. Instead, she had remained as prim as a maiden aunt and ironically this had only increased his hunger for her. His mouth dried. As if he needed any more hunger than was already coursing around his frustrated veins!

'So you've got what you wanted,' she observed thoughtfully.

A pulse flickered at his temple as she tilted her chin with faint challenge. 'On the contrary, Jazz,' he demurred softly. 'I'm still waiting for the thing I want most.'

Her eyes narrowed as she looked at him and suddenly all that old sexual shorthand was back. The flush to her cheeks and the darkening of her eyes. The spring of her nipples against the silk of her robes and quick writhe of the hips, which was almost imperceptible to anyone else but him.

'Jazz,' he said, on a throaty note of hunger he couldn't disguise and he heard her answering intake of breath. Did she move first or did he, and wasn't that something he needed to know—in order to establish whose victory this was? But suddenly Zuhal didn't care—not about the method, only the result. He didn't care which of them had backed down as, with a hungry moan, he closed his arms around her and desire reverberated through him as never before.

Her mouth opened beneath his kiss and her moan echoed his as he explored her with his tongue. Sweet heaven, but she tasted good. So good. His shaking hands were on her robes, tugging at them impatiently with none of his usual restraint, and she was doing the same thing to him—touching his body through the delicate material as if she were discovering it for the very first time. But this was nothing like the first time. Back then she had been a virgin and now she was a sexually experienced woman who knew exactly what she wanted. And so did he.

Her hand pressed boldly against his erection as he deepened the kiss and, urgently, he backed her up against the wall, peeling off her tunic and flinging it aside before dispensing with his own the same way. He ripped off her panties so that they fluttered onto the Persian rug, his fingers quickly finding the moist heat now exposed to him and beginning a deliciously familiar rhythm. The scent of sex filled the air as he strummed against the warm syrupy feel of her and she bucked immediately.

'Yes,' she gasped, brokenly, and suddenly she forgot everything. Forgot that she probably shouldn't be doing this and that Zuhal wasn't using any protection. All she could think about was it. And him. The word burst out of her lips again. 'Yes.'

His hands clamped around the cool flesh of her buttocks, he lifted her up so she could lock her thighs around his hips, positioning herself perfectly for that first, deep thrust which made her gasp in the way he remembered so well For a moment he had to still in order to compose himself, terrified he would come straight away—like some over-keen schoolboy whose wildest fantasy had just been realised.

'*Oh*,' he breathed, as control returned to him and he resumed his thrust. Each. Hard. Hungry. Thrust. 'Isn't that good, Jazz?' he demanded unsteadily. 'Isn't it the best thing you ever felt?'

Her breath was hot against his neck, her words slurred with pleasure. 'Is it praise you're seeking, Zuhal?'

No, it wasn't praise. He told himself it was orgasm he wanted—all he had ever wanted—but orgasms were easily attained, weren't they? And then he stopped thinking altogether, focussing instead on how tight she felt as his balls slapped softly against her molten heat. On how his heart was pounding like a regimental drum as he increased his speed. He drove into her while doing all the things he knew she liked best. Grazing her nipples with his teeth—so that she was balancing on the fine edge between pain and pleasure. Stroking his thumb down the enticing valley which cleaved between her buttocks, so that she moaned softly with pleasure.

When she came, he followed almost immediately, kissing away her shuddering moans as his seed spurted long and deep into her body and he felt the inexplicable clench of his heart. Long minutes passed as her head flopped against his shoulder and he could hear her breathing fanning his neck. At last she unfolded her legs and slid them down so that she was standing again, her weight now pressed against the wall instead of into his body. But when he tilted her chin to stare into her eyes, she was having none of it and shook her head.

'No. Don't say anything,' she said.

'Not even to ask you whether you'd like to do it all over again?'

Her emerald gaze was very clear. 'And if I did, would you use some protection this time?'

He nodded. 'Of course I would. I wasn't thinking. At least, not about that.'

There was a fraction of a pause. 'Neither was I. But I need to do some thinking now, so will you please go?' She shook her head as if to pre-empt further argument. 'I mean it, Zuhal. Just go.'

It took a moment or two for him to realise she meant it and slowly he expelled a long breath. It was the first time he'd ever been ejected from a woman's bedroom but to Zuhal it suddenly felt more like a reprieve than a punishment. Because wasn't it a relief to be spared the inevitable analysis of what had just happened, in that tedious way women had of always overthinking things?

They both knew exactly what had just happened.

Sex. Amazing sex—nothing more and nothing less.

His lips curved into a satisfied smile as he allowed himself the brief luxury of a stretch. 'Sure,' he said, as he bent to retrieve his discarded robes.

CHAPTER TEN

THE SUN WAS rising in the dawn sky as Zuhal headed towards the stables next morning. He felt the tension leaching from his body—something he attributed to the amazing sex he'd had with Jazz last night, an erotic encounter which was making him grow hard just thinking about it. Because tension was an integral part of his life now, he recognised. It went hand in hand with the many new challenges facing him as monarch. Yet he found himself relishing those challenges in a way he hadn't been anticipating, because he had never imagined he would be King. To rule had never been his destiny, but already his people were beginning to accept him, even to warm to him, and he was confident that he would be able to do his best by them.

Wasn't that the silver lining to the dark cloud which had descended on him when

Kamal had disappeared? The realisation that he no longer felt the outsider in the country of his birth?

The distant sky was a flamboyant display of flamingo-pink and orange as he swung himself into the saddle and urged his horse forward. Last night had been pivotal in all kinds of ways. He had spent the evening watching Jazz perform admirably as Queen-in-Waiting and her subsequent sexual capitulation boded well for the future. Surely now there was no further barrier stopping him from making her his bride? No reason for her to keep him dangling while she tantalisingly refused to give him her answer.

His mouth curved into a speculative smile. He remembered the way he had ripped the robes from her body and the way she had moaned as his fingers found her wet heat. Pride was all very well, but sexual satisfaction was a far more powerful motivator. Wouldn't that fast and furious encounter encourage her to go ahead with the marriage as quickly as possible, so that they could become husband and wife?

He rode for nearly an hour and was galloping back towards the stables when, suddenly, he caught sight of the gleam of blonde hair in the distance. Jazz. He felt his groin tighten as his gaze drank her in. In the light desert breeze, the folds of her robes had moulded themselves to her delectable body and he was reminded of clasping those luscious curves before bringing them both to orgasm. Was she eager for an early replay? he thought with hungry amusement Was that why she was here? Perhaps she wanted him to tumble her onto the stable floor and take her amid all the bales of hay, rutting into her like a stallion?

'So this time you don't mind being seen?' he questioned as he slowed his horse and drew up beside her.

She blinked up at him in alarm. 'Seen?'

He jumped down onto the dusty ground. 'Didn't I once observe you watching me from afar? Standing in a corner of the stables and watching while I took off my clothes?' Her answering colour told him that her shadowed presence hadn't been a figment of his overheated imagination and, although she was now glaring at him, he smiled. 'Don't worry, I rather liked you in the role of voyeur.'

'I'm not worried!' she flared back at him, her cheeks still flushed and pink.

'So why are you here?' he mused softly. 'As far as I'm aware, we aren't supposed to be meeting for another hour and I need to shower first. Unless what happened last night means you're thinking you might like to join me? I'm quite happy for you to soap me off, my beauty. It's far too long since we had a shower together.'

Jasmine wished he would stop making sexual allusions every time he opened his mouth because they were drawing her attention to his body, which she'd been trying very hard to forget. But how could she forget when the memory had kept her awake most of the night, as she'd recalled the way he had driven into her. Her cheeks grew hotter as she remembered her eagerness to have sex with him—backed up against one of the palace walls, of all places, with her legs wrapped tightly around his bare back as he had taken her on a quick trip to paradise. What had happened to her determination to keep things on an impartial footing until she had discovered whether she wanted to marry him? It had vanished the moment he had taken her in his arms and kissed her.

'I don't want to talk about that,' she said. 'Last night shouldn't have happened.'

His eyes glittered. 'Are you quite sure?'

'Quite sure. I'm supposed to be getting to know you,' she continued. 'In a rather more formal way than that.'

'As you wish. I've never had to beg a woman for sex before, Jazz—and I'm certainly not going to start now.'

'It was usually the other way round, was it?' she queried mischievously.

He gave a brief smile as they began to walk towards the stables, and Jasmine suddenly became aware of a sense of wistfulness as she breathed in a long-forgotten fragrance. 'I love that smell,' she said suddenly.

He turned to look at her. 'What smell?'

'You know. Horses. Leather. Dust. Sweat. The whole thing. Stables, I guess.' She gave a sigh, which seemed to bubble up out of nowhere. 'You're very lucky to be able to ride out in the desert with no fences or houses or roads to get in the way. You must get a real sense of freedom out here—the kind you don't really get back in England.'

He narrowed his eyes, as one of the grooms led his horse away. 'You sound as if you know what you're talking about.'

'You seem surprised.'

'Maybe I am. I thought you were the quint-essential city girl. Are you telling me you can ride, Jazz?'

'Yes, I can ride,' she said quietly. 'I used to love all things equestrian until the age of ten. Or did you think I'd always been poor and that riding is a rich person's sport?'

He lifted his hand by a fraction, but the quirk of his lips indicated a signal of acknowledgement rather than command.

'So what happened when you were ten?' he continued curiously as they began to walk back towards the palace.

Jasmine tried to avert her gaze from the thrust of his thighs against his jodhpurs, but it wasn't easy—particularly when she thought of her fingers roving over their hair-roughened power last night and the memory of what lay at their apex. She cleared her throat. 'It was a continuation of the fallen-ice-cream episode,' she said.

'The fallen ice cream?' he repeated blankly.

'You remember. I told you about it in London. When my father left home.' She gave an impatient shake of her shoulders. 'Weren't you listening?'

'Yes, of course I was listening. Forgive me. I

am feeling a little *distracted*. You can't blame me for that, in view of what happened between us last night.' With what looked like an effort, he dragged his gaze from her torso to her face. 'So what happened—after your father left home?'

He had stopped walking and was looking at her, waiting for her answer.

'We had to sell the house and the car,' she explained. 'And my pony was the first thing to go, obviously.'

'Why?'

Jasmine felt a flicker of irritation at his incomprehension. Did he really lack the imagination to work it out for himself, or was he just incapable of putting himself into the shoes of a normal person? She stared down at her feet, aware of a fine layer of dust from the yard which was now covering her toes and wishing she'd worn something more substantial than beaded flip-flops.

She lifted her gaze to his. 'Because as well as making his much younger secretary pregnant and causing a scandal at work, my father had also been living beyond his means—and once it was discovered, everything started to tumble down. The banks needed to be paid and there was no money to pay them. It meant my mum was left with very little. In fact, with almost nothing. We had to start renting a tiny apartment.' She sucked in a deep breath. 'And Mum had to go back out to work—but the only work she could get was cleaning. Overnight she went from being a middle-class wife to what she called a "skivvy" and she never got over it, really. She got ill soon after that. Perhaps the two things were related.'

Zuhal met the sombre expression clouding her green-gold eyes. It must have been tough, he acknowledged, as they resumed their step and the soaring blue cupolas of the palace swam into view. Maybe everyone's childhood was tough, he concluded grimly as several servants spotted him and lowered their gazes in natural deference. Or maybe it was family life itself which created all the problems. He thought about his own parents. About the so-called 'love' which had corrupted the atmosphere with so much poison. His mouth twisted. Who needed it? Surely mutual tolerance and good sex were a better long-term bet than all the chaos wreaked by love?

He observed the glint of sunlight on Jazz's pale hair and imagined her as a horse-mad young girl. He could picture her in a smart jacket, her hair in a net and a crop in her hand. A bright rosette pinned to her pony as she leaned forward to pat the forelock. It must have hurt to have lost all that, he realised with a sudden flash of insight, which wasn't usually his thing. Because although he didn't have quite the same affinity with horses as his brother did—*had done*—he corrected painfully, he still valued his daily ride above most things.

'Would you like to ride out with me tomorrow morning?' he said as she began to move away from him.

She turned back and he could see the uncertainty on her face. 'I haven't been on a horse for years,' she said. 'I don't know if I can still do it.'

'There's only one way to find out.'

'I don't know, Zuhal.'

'Is that a yes?' he prompted softly, and suddenly it mattered. It mattered a lot.

There was a pause and then she nodded, her blonde ponytail shimmering like the tail of a horse in the early-morning haze as her green eyes met his. 'It's a yes. And thank you. But there's no way I'll be able to keep up with you.

Give me the most gentle horse in your stable and I'll be happy just trotting around the yard.'

'You will do no such thing,' he vowed. 'You can have my undivided teaching skills, if you like.' He felt the flicker of a pulse at his temple and the more insistent one which was throbbing deep in his groin. 'And don't they say it all comes rushing back, the moment you're back in the saddle?'

'I guess they do,' she said and the smile she gave him lingered long after he had watched her retreating into the palace.

He spent longer in the shower than usual—mainly because his newly ignited sexual hunger refused to be doused, even by the prolonged jets of icy water over his heated skin. He found himself bemused and intrigued by her determination to ignore what had happened last night. Unless her prudishness was all for show and she was planning to seduce him during their ten o'clock appointment in the Damask Room. Yes, that could work. That could work very well. He felt the flicker of a pulse at his temple and ordered Adham to ensure that he was not disturbed for the duration of the meeting, telling him it was possible it might run over.

But his anticipation was dampened the moment Jazz was shown into the room and he saw a new light of purpose glinting from her green-gold eyes. She was wearing a demure cream gown which covered her from head to ankle and his heart sank. Sinking down gracefully into one of the soft chairs, she pressed her knees together and he couldn't help contrasting her demure image with the wildcat lover who had greedily met his urgent thrusts last night.

'I'd like to discuss bringing the high chair into the dining room,' she began, without any kind of fanfare.

He narrowed his eyes. 'Excuse me?'

'I think it's best if we make some attempt to live as a normal family, even if these surroundings are far from normal, and neither is our situation. But I think it would benefit Darius if he joined us at lunchtime. That's all.'

Zuhal frowned. 'Have you forgotten that we often have international delegations with officials present during lunch?' he demanded.

'No, I haven't forgotten. But it will do them good to see the powerful King living as other men do. It would make you seem more...approachable.'

'You think I'm unapproachable?' he demanded.

She hesitated. 'I think as King you're still an unknown factor and interacting with your son will show people a softer side of you. Can you see any reason why we shouldn't give it a trial run, Zuhal?'

He met the determination in her eyes and felt a smile begin to build. 'I guess not,' he said, as grudging admiration for her sheer tenacity washed over him.

Then followed a debate about the installation of a small sandpit—'It's not as if we're short of the raw material, Zuhal!'—and before he knew it the half-hour was up. The meeting had not gone as he had hoped and yet, for some reason, he found himself whistling softly underneath his breath as he went off to his next appointment.

Next morning she joined him at the stables and he discovered that she was a good rider who possessed a natural affinity with the horse he had chosen especially for her. At first their routes were slow and unambitious—rarely venturing too far from the palace, until Zuhal was confident that Jazz herself was at ease. He watched her walk and canter and gallop with a growing feeling of satisfaction. He observed her increasing confidence as she and the horse became better acquainted before increasing the scope of their rides by taking her a little further into the desert.

And the stream of questions she'd implied she'd wanted the answers to had somehow failed to materialise. Maybe the sheer physicality of riding demanded all her attention, or maybe she was cleverer than he'd given her credit for by not pushing him into a corner. Her occasional queries were light—like butterflies dropping onto a blossom rather than rocks falling into a well. They seemed to encourage confidences rather than making him clam up, as had happened so often in the past whenever women had tried to delve beneath the surface. Once or twice, he found himself offering an opinion which hadn't been asked for. Like the time he'd admitted missing the banter and friendly rivalry he'd shared with his brother. Or confessing that being a ruler was harder than he'd envisaged and perhaps he had judged Kamal too harshly—something which troubled him now. He didn't tell her that for the first time ever he felt as if his life had true meaning. That he was no longer just the royal 'spare', and as ruler he found he had the power to make a difference.

But after an entire fortnight of uneventful rides, Zuhal had decided that enough was enough. He wanted her in his arms again and her body language was sending out a silent message that she wanted him just as much. This celibate existence had gone on long enough. He would put her in a position where she couldn't distract herself with horses or babies and this time *demand* she marry him!

The ride they embarked on the following day was their most ambitious yet and for most of it he rode beside her, his headdress streaming in the wind as they tracked the golden sands in silence, the pounding of hooves and the snort of the horses the only sounds to be heard.

'Look over there,' he said after a while, slowing down to point into the distance. 'See anything?'

Screwing up her eyes, Jasmine noticed a tiny dot on the horizon which was growing bigger as they rode towards it, until she saw the outline of a large tent with a conical roof. Nearby was an unexpected copse of trees and a group of smaller tents. In the shade of the trees they dismounted and Zuhal tethered the horses before two male servants appeared from one of the smaller tents, bringing bowls of water for the animals to drink.

'Is this what you call an oasis?'

'Ten out of ten, Jazz,' he murmured.

He motioned for her to follow him into the cool interior of the largest tent, which stood some distance away. Dipping her head to enter, she gave an audible gasp as she gazed around the deceptively vast interior where intricate bronze lamps hung from the ceiling and silken rugs were scattered over the floor. A large day-bed of silver brocade stood beside an exquisitely carved table, on which reposed tiny glasses studded with the rainbow colours of what looked like real jewels.

'Oh, Zuhal—it's beautiful,' she breathed, unable to conceal her wonder or her delight. 'I don't think I've ever seen anything quite so beautiful.'

'Not even at the Granchester Hotel,' he questioned sarcastically.

A smile played at the edges of her lips. 'Not even there!'

He inclined his head in acknowledgement. 'Please, sit,' he said formally.

A little saddle-sore after the long ride, Jasmine obeyed, sinking into the heap of cushions he was indicating, while Zuhal called out something in his own language before lowering himself down beside her.

'What is this place?' she asked, as one of the servants appeared at the door of the tent, bearing a large stone jug and dispensing cool liquid into two tiny jewelled glasses.

'It is my refuge,' he said slowly, once the servant had left. 'It was my brother's refuge too, and our father's before him. It is traditionally the place where kings have come to escape from the pressures of court and palace life.'

Jasmine nodded as she took a sip of the refreshing drink. She had been treading on eggshells for days, afraid of driving him away with her curiosity and trying to establish some kind of trust between them, but something told her that now was the time to dig a little deeper. 'What was it like?' she asked, putting her glass down and leaning back against the soft nest of cushions.

'What?' he queried obliquely.

'Growing up in a palace.'

'You've experienced something of that

yourself,' he answered carelessly. 'You will have noted the presence of servants. Of days which are governed by form and by structure. Of the innate need for formality—despite your single-handed mission to disrupt that formality by having our son eat his lunch with us.'

Jazz felt an inner glow because it was the first time he'd ever said *our* son. 'You can't deny that he's been very well behaved!' she defended.

'No, I cannot deny that,' he agreed gravely.

There was a pause before, encouraged by his relaxed demeanour, she asked a little more. 'So how did being a royal impact on your family, when you were a child?'

He shrugged. 'I never knew anything different. My blood is blue on both sides. My father came from a long line of desert kings and my mother was a princess from the neighbouring country of Israqan.'

Her voice was cautious. 'So was it an arranged marriage?'

'Unfortunately, no. It was not,' he answered repressively. 'If it had been there might have been a chance it might have worked. As it was, they met at the Razrastanian embassy in New York and *fell in love*.'

Jasmine registered the unmistakable contempt which had coloured those last three words. 'And was that so bad?'

'It was disastrous,' he said, his lips twisting with derision. 'Experience has taught me that love is nothing but an illusion which justifies desire and such...*passion* cannot possibly be sustained. At first it is an explosion—but explosions inevitably destroy whatever is around them. And then there is drama. Endless drama—with scenes and fights and tears. How I hate drama,' he added bitterly.

'And is that what happened—to your parents?'

'That is exactly what happened.' His black eyes glittered. 'It quickly burnt itself out and all that was left were two people who were essentially incompatible and who hated one another.'

'I'm sorry to hear that,' she offered, pausing for a moment before asking, 'So how did they deal with it?'

Again, he shrugged. 'My father sought comfort elsewhere and my mother threw all her energies into preparing my brother for his accession to the throne, in order to make him the finest ruler this land has ever known.'

'Did she indulge him?' she asked sharply.

'You could say that.' He took a last mouthful of juice before putting the jewelled beaker down. 'He grew up feeling he was capable of anything. That he was indestructible.'

'And where did you come in all this?' she questioned suddenly. 'Where did you fit in, Zuhal?'

Zuhal's eyes narrowed. Perceptive of her. But also perhaps a little too close to the bone. He prepared to bat away her question with flippancy before something stopped him and he frowned as he became aware that he had never admitted this to anyone. He'd never really been in a position to before, because he hadn't seen the point in confiding in any of his lovers, knowing that to do so would have been a potential security breach.

Yet suddenly the desire to connect was stronger than his innate desire to conceal. Was that because, as his potential wife, Jazz needed to know what kind of man he really was—so she didn't foster any unrealistic fantasies which could never be met? 'I didn't fit in anywhere,' he grated. 'Not then. I was the forgotten son. The invisible son. There's no need to look so shocked, Jazz. Don't they say every mother has her favourite? Well, it wasn't me. But I was well fed and well cared for and that was enough.' He saw the pain in her eyes and reached out to tilt her chin with his finger. 'Have I told you enough for one day? Don't you find the discussion of dysfunction a little…tedious? Surely you can think of a more pleasurable way of passing the time other than talking about a past which is lost to us for ever?'

The air between them thrummed. The breath left her lungs. Glancing up into the inky gleam of his eyes, Jasmine felt an erratic quickening of her pulse. She wanted to know more but she sensed that now was not the time, just as she sensed that Zuhal needed her now in a way he hadn't needed her before.

'I can think of several things,' she said huskily. 'It depends which one you're referring to.'

'You know exactly what I'm talking about.' He sprung to his feet to close the tent flaps, so that the interior instantly grew dim and mysterious. Now the cavernous space was lit only by the silvery brocade of the day-bed, the silky colours of the rugs and the bright sheen of metal lamps as he returned to join her on the floor and pulled her into his arms again. 'This,' he breathed. 'I'm talking about this.'

Jasmine knew he was going to kiss her but underpinning her desire was an overwhelming rush of emotion as he put his arms around her, as she thought about the little boy who nobody had wanted. But then he sank her into the soft cushions and her thoughts were forgotten as their mouths met in a hard and hungry kiss which left them gasping for oxygen.

His fingers were unsteady as he unbuttoned her shirt and tugged it from her shoulders, so that she was lying there in just her jodhpurs, riding boots and a black lacy bra. 'That's better,' he murmured.

'Do you—?'

'No. No more words, Jazz,' he said, with a shake of his head as he bent to pull off her riding boots. The jodhpurs were next to go, each movement a sensual torture as he slowly stroked them down her thighs, his fingers whispering tantalisingly over the black lace wisp of her panties. She gasped as he unclipped her straining bra, so that her breasts spilled out—one nipple finding itself positioned perfectly for his waiting lips to suck on.

'Oh!' she gasped.

'I thought I said no words.'

'I couldn't help myself.'

His eyes swept over her, as he swiftly removed his own clothes before taking her hand in his. 'Is this what you want?' he questioned, directing her fingertips to his groin. 'I think it is. It's certainly what *I* want.'

And Jasmine needed no further guidance as she wrapped her trembling fingers around his mighty shaft, enjoying the sound of his murmured pleasure as she began to slide them up and down the silken skin. Lying down beside her, he kissed her until she was quivering—touching every inch of her with a taunting skill, until she was making strangled little pleas. At last he positioned himself over her and she could feel the heaviness of his body and the hard brush of his erection between her thighs. And then he gave one hard, long thrust, to tunnel up deep inside her—and as he did so, another rush of emotion threatened to overwhelm her. Closing her eyes, Jasmine sank her lips against his sweat-sheened shoulder. Because this wasn't some *wham-bam* bout up against the wall. This was heart-stoppingly intimate and terrifying in its implications. And only Zuhal could make her feel like this. Respond like this.

'Zuhal,' she said brokenly, but maybe he

didn't hear. Maybe he was so intent on giving her pleasure that he was oblivious to her turbulent feelings—or maybe he just preferred to ignore them. And then everything was forgotten as her body began to spasm helplessly around him.

She was dimly aware of the choked cry he gave as her back arched and the spurting rush as he filled her with his seed. When the world came back into focus at last, it was for her to find his dark head resting on her breast, one bent arm around her neck, his breath warm against her damp skin. And wasn't it infuriating how stupidly *mushy* she felt? Wasn't she in danger of falling for him all over again, despite his emotional distance and his obvious mistrust of anything to do with love? But then something occurred to her—something which drove all these thoughts clean from her mind.

'That's the second time we've omitted to use any protection,' she said.

He stirred and yawned. 'Doing it with you as nature intended just seems to come naturally to me,' he admitted. 'Do you mind?'

Jasmine hesitated, aware that something had shifted and changed between them. Say it, she urged herself. Don't expect him to guess what you're thinking and then be angry when he gets it wrong. 'I think it's better if we decide if and when to have another baby,' she said carefully. 'Rather than just leaving it to chance.'

'Do you want another baby, Jazz?'

There was a long segment of silence. 'If we're to be married, then yes, I think I do,' she answered eventually.

'You mean the marriage you've been dragging your feet about?'

She didn't deny his accusation, just shifted her weight a little as she looked up into his eyes. 'Because up until now, we've seemed more like strangers than anything else.'

His black gaze burned into her. 'But now we're no longer "strangers"—you're happy for it to go ahead?'

Happy? It seemed a strange word to use in the circumstances. It felt a long time since she'd experienced that particular emotion. When she'd found herself alone and pregnant, it had been independence which Jasmine had strived for and, against all the odds, she had achieved it. Even though it had been a bit of a struggle, she had forged a decent life for herself and Darius. She had been her own woman—in charge of her own destiny—and she recognised that her growing feelings for Zuhal threatened to destabilise everything she had achieved.

She met the dark gleam of his eyes. Yet today he had shown a chink in his armour and a vulnerability she hadn't expected. He'd described the awful atmosphere in the palace when he'd been growing up. He'd described how his parents had made a mockery of love and how he despised and mistrusted the word and all it stood for as a consequence. She got that. But she could show him by example that it didn't need to be like that, couldn't she? She loved Darius and maybe Zuhal would come to realise that love wasn't always a dirty word. And if that happened, then couldn't they learn to love each other—or was that a wish too far?

'Yes,' she said gravely. 'I am. And I'm prepared to give our marriage my very best shot.'

'Good.' He inclined his dark head. 'Then it is agreed. We will wed as soon as possible. We will become husband and wife and have shared goals for a stable future, not just for the monarchy, but for Darius—and for any brothers and sisters he may have.'

She thought how business-like they both sounded—as if they were dealing with a business merger rather than a relationship. But his mouth was soft as he reached out for her and most of her misgivings melted away beneath the sensual onslaught of another heady kiss.

She kissed him back with a fervour which matched his own and his face was tight as he lifted her up and brought her down onto his aching shaft, groaning as she began to ride him. And suddenly it was all happening so fast. Indecently fast. She felt that first sweet clench which began to dominate her world as she began to come, aware that he was watching her closely. His fingers were tight on her breasts as her back arched and she threw her head back with a fierce shout which was quickly echoed by his own.

Afterwards they lay there very quietly, and it was with a beat of something which felt like hope for the future that Jasmine agreed to Zuhal's suggestion that they head back to the palace. With a sense of torpor, they dressed and drank some juice before going back outside, where the rested horses seemed infected by their laziness, making the return ride slow and leisurely.

Zuhal wasn't quite sure at which point he noticed that something was different. Was it the barely perceptible flash from one of the palace windows, as if someone was looking out for them, which made his body grow tense? Or was it just the sight of three of his aides waiting for them in the stable yard—Adham among them, which was highly unusual?

There was an expression on his chief aide's face which he'd never seen before—one he couldn't quite decipher—and Zuhal's heart gave a lurch of foreboding as he tried to work out exactly what was going on. But then he saw a rare smile break out on Adham's face as he rushed forward to greet the Sheikh.

'Your Royal Highness!' exclaimed the aide, not even waiting until Zuhal had leapt from his horse. 'I have wondrous news! Your brother is returned. The King is alive!'

CHAPTER ELEVEN

'WHERE THE HELL have you been?'

Zuhal stared into the face of his brother—a brother he hardly recognised. Kamal's face was gaunt, his eyes sunken, and his ragged clothes unlike any he would usually wear as royal regalia. He must have lost at least twenty pounds, and his black hair flowed down past his shoulders. Only his proud deportment betrayed the fact that this was no ordinary man who had been lost in the desert for months and months, but in fact a desert king.

'Well?' Zuhal's demand rang out through the echoing Throne Room. The blonde gleam of Jasmine's hair reminded him she was sitting in the window seat, but he barely noticed her—his only focus on the brother he had thought was dead. Utter relief at seeing his only sibling alive suddenly transformed itself into righteous anger. 'Are you going to give me some kind of explanation about how you've just miraculously returned, after we've spent months sending search parties out for you?'

Kamal nodded, his gaunt expression becoming tight and tense, as if he had no desire to relive what had happened to him. 'The sandstorm came down on us suddenly and my horse and I were lost—'

'That much I know,' Zuhal interrupted impatiently. 'And if you'd bothered letting someone know where you were going then we could have found you.'

'No. You could never have found me,' said Kamal, his voice suddenly bleak. 'For I was swallowed up in the most inaccessible part of the desert, heavily concussed, with my leg broken.'

'Oh, my brother,' said Zuhal, his voice suddenly trembling with an emotion he did not recognise.

'Were it not for the nomadic tribe from the Harijia region who found me and took me in and helped me back to health, I would surely have died.' Kamal looked down at his hands. 'I lived in their tents as one of them for many months and they taught me much about the land I thought I knew. I liked living there.' He lifted his gaze to his brother. 'For a while I thought I wanted to stay. Maybe a part of me didn't want to come back and continue to be King.'

There was a silence.

'So what changed your mind?' asked Zuhal slowly.

There was silence. 'I heard you were getting married to the Englishwoman.' Another pause. 'And that she had a child.'

Noiselessly Jasmine rose to her feet and left the Throne Room, but nobody noticed her go. Of course they didn't. Ever since they'd returned to the palace she'd felt invisible to the man she'd spent the afternoon having sex with and the reason for that was as plain as the nose on her face. The King had returned and her place here was now redundant.

An exhausted Kamal retired early and Jasmine spent that night in Zuhal's bed, but his lovemaking—although satisfying—felt almost *perfunctory* and he resolutely refused to discuss the impact of the King's return on their future. The following morning he had already left for his early ride when she woke and Jasmine was aware of a sharp sense of disappointment that he hadn't taken her with him, as was usual. Had he only tolerated her accompanying him on his daily ride because he'd wanted her to marry him?

But now there was no longer any need for him to marry her, was there?

Jasmine found herself in a strange position. She felt alone and scared—more scared even than when she'd found herself pregnant. She didn't want to put any more pressure on Zuhal but this sense of being in limbo wasn't doing her any good. She needed to face up to the facts and calmly ask the Sheikh what he really wanted now that his brother had returned— perhaps when they were in bed, soft and satiated by sex. Perhaps when her arms were around his waist and he was nuzzling her neck in a way which made her shiver with something deeper than desire. Or would it be easier if they were face to face across a table, so that she wasn't naked and vulnerable? So that she could calmly get up and leave and go and cry with dignity and in private...

Trying to work out the best way to approach such a delicate matter, she took Darius out for an afternoon stroll, planning to sit in the palace rose garden and sing him the soft lullabies he loved. Rainbow light arced through the spray of the ornate fountains, and the blousy blooms of perfumed flowers made her feel as if she'd tumbled into a kaleidoscopic fantasy-land as she walked through the spacious gardens. She was going to miss this beautiful place, she thought, with a sudden clench of her heart.

The air was soft and drowsy with the buzz of bees and Jasmine thought she heard the drift of voices coming from the interior of the rose garden. She wondered who it might be as her sandaled feet moved silently towards the sound, until the familiar velvety caress of her lover's voice indicated he was deep in conversation with his brother.

She didn't mean to eavesdrop. In fact, she was just about to turn away and go somewhere else in order to give them peace, when she heard her name mentioned. She told herself afterwards that it was only human nature to stand there for a moment or two. To want to know what was being said about her. She told herself it was a good thing she *did* listen—because otherwise, how would she have known the truth? Wouldn't she just have carried on weaving impossible dreams about the future and hoping that one day Zuhal might learn to love her, if only a little?

'Jazz?' Zuhal's voice was drawling. 'What about her?'

'Won't she mind not being Queen—now that I'm back?'

'It is not in her remit to *mind*.'

'But she is a woman, Zuhal—and women are notoriously ambitious for their men.'

'Not Jazz.' There was a pause. 'We don't have that kind of relationship.'

'What kind of relationship *do* you have, then?'

'It defies definition,' said Zuhal flippantly.

'Oh?' Kamal's voice probed further. 'Are you still going to marry her, now that I'm back?'

'I haven't decided.'

Jasmine bristled at his arrogance—his innate certainty that *he* was the one who called the shots—when Kamal's next question made her heart pound violently against her breastbone.

'Do you love her?'

There was another pause, during which Jasmine could hear some unknown bird singing high from one of the treetops, and its sweet, drenching song sounded unbearably poignant.

'No,' said Zuhal, in a hard, empty voice. 'You must realise by now that I don't do love, Kamal.'

She'd known that all along, but even so Jasmine was surprised by the fierce intensity of the pain which ripped through her as she registered that cold and unequivocal statement. She wanted to gasp with shock and pain—but somehow she held it back, because now was not the time. And really, she'd learned nothing new, had she? Because nothing had changed.

Zuhal had told her he didn't do love. He mistrusted it and didn't want it—for reasons which were perfectly understandable. He'd told her that emphatically and now he was stating it loud and clear to his brother. Perhaps he was doing her a favour. Would she really have been content to spend her life here with him, not daring to show her feelings for fear it would make him angry, or suspicious that she had started to love him again? What kind of an example would that set to Darius?

She was trembling as she silently turned the pram and pushed it away as fast as she dared go, knowing that there was only one solution which lay open to her—and she took the baby to Rania, before going to Zuhal's offices to find him. Ignoring Adham's protest, she walked straight into the Sheikh's office without knocking to find him talking on the phone. Something in her face must have sent out an unspoken warning because he uttered a few terse words in his native tongue before terminating the call and rising slowly to his feet.

'This is unexpected,' he said, a faint note of reproof in his deep voice.

'I overheard you,' she said.

His brow darkened. 'What are you talking about?'

'In the garden, talking to your brother. I heard you say you didn't love me.'

He didn't look in the slightest bit abashed. 'But you knew that already, Jazz. I've never lied to you about that.'

'No, I know you haven't.' She drew in a deep breath. 'And while part of me respects you for your honesty, I've realised I can't live like that. It's not good for our son to live like that either.'

'So what do you expect me to say in response

to this?' he demanded. 'To tell you that I didn't mean it?'

'No. I don't expect that, Zuhal. If you must know I admire your honesty and the fact that you've never spun out lies or empty promises.' She took a deep breath. 'But I just want you to arrange for me and Darius to return to England, and as soon as possible.'

He raised his dark brows. 'To do what?'

She shrugged. 'To live somewhere—not London, but close enough for you to be able to access us easily. And a house, I think—not an apartment—because I want Darius to have a garden of his own. I'd like to go back to Oxfordshire until I can find something which meets with your approval. You can even appoint your bodyguards if you wish—since I recognise that as Darius is your son we need protection. But I want to go back, Zuhal.' Her voice suddenly became low. Urgent. 'And as soon as possible.'

Zuhal's mouth hardened with anger and contempt as he acknowledged Jazz's manipulative demands. Well, if she was hoping he would start grovelling in an attempt to persuade her to stay, then she was in for a disappointment. He didn't argue with her, because this kind of conversation felt like one he'd had too often with women in the past—though never with Jazz, he conceded. It was emotional blackmail. She was making a statement. She was leaving.

And she was taking their son with her.

He kept his cold resolve through all the arrangements for their departure and maintained it as he saw her and Darius off from the airfield. But he couldn't deny the inexplicable lurch of his heart as he saw her disappearing inside the private jet, his son's dark curly head bobbing over her shoulder. It felt as if a dark cloud were descending on him as he recalled saying goodbye to his child, who'd naturally been too young to realise what was happening. But *he* had known, hadn't he? Had known and felt guilty and resentful, all at the same time—half tempted to tell Jazz that he wouldn't allow her to take his progeny from the country, but knowing deep down that the child needed his mother.

The powerful engines roared but he turned away so that his back was to the plane during take-off, mainly because he'd got a damned speck of dust in his eye and infuriatingly, it was watering. On returning to the palace, he worked solidly for the rest of the day, checking his phone with unusual regularity.

But the only thing he heard from Jazz was after she'd touched down in England and sent a miserable little text saying, I'm back. Which, of course, he had already known, because his security people had alerted him.

He sent back an equally bald text:

I will be in touch to discuss arrangements about Darius.

But she didn't reply, which infuriated him even more.

His handover to Kamal almost complete, he decided to reward himself with some extra riding, deciding that some hard physical exercise was exactly what he needed to rid himself of this strange frustration which was burning away inside him. But for once the exertion and beauty of the desert failed to work their magic and he realised he was missing Darius more than he would ever have imagined. His mouth thinned. He would travel to Europe and see him, but he would do it in his own time and on *his* terms.

Stopping in Paris en route for a long-overdue meeting, he checked himself into a sybaritically indulgent hotel with glittering views over the river Seine, for an overnight stay. He wasn't really in the mood for socialising but unexpectedly ran into the dashing ex-polo player, Alejandro Sabato, and agreed to have dinner with him. He'd forgotten how the charismatic Argentinean attracted women like wasps buzzing towards uncovered food and several times their meal was interrupted while one of them gushingly requested a selfie with the ex-world champion. And then, much to Zuhal's annoyance, they were papped leaving the upmarket restaurant.

Zuhal's eyes were gritty when he woke next morning and, although he tried ringing Jazz from his plane before he touched down in England, the call went straight to voicemail. But she didn't bother ringing back and neither did she pick up the second call he made as his limousine—with diplomatic flag flying—sped from the airfield towards Oxfordshire.

A house had been purchased for her, not far from where she'd lived before—but her new home was a world away from her old, rented cottage. Set like a jewel in an acre of walled garden, the detached villa had mullioned windows which glinted like diamonds in the sunshine and a soft grey front door. Two bright pots of scarlet geraniums stood on either side of the front door and the sporty little saloon he'd insisted on buying for her was parked in front of the garage. But when Zuhal lifted the shiny bronze knocker to sound out a summons through the house, nobody came to the door. He tried again with the same result and he scowled.

Where the hell *was* she?

His anger grew as he waited in his limousine, drumming his fingers against his knees and glancing out at the lonely lane, wondering if she was safe and wondering why he had allowed her to live this kind of existence in the English countryside. By the time she returned, a bag bulging with groceries on the bottom of the pram, he was seething, as his eyes raked over her.

She was back to wearing jeans and a shirt, and her hair was twisted into a plait as she returned his gaze with shuttered eyes. She couldn't have looked less like the perfumed Queen she'd been poised to become, yet something twisted deep inside him as he stared at her. Something he didn't want to acknowledge for fear of where it would take him.

'Wouldn't it be more sensible to have one of the bodyguards do your shopping for you?' he demanded, as he carefully helped her manoeuvre the pram into the spacious hallway of the house to avoid waking the baby. 'Rather than struggling like this on your own?'

'Not if I want to have any semblance of living a normal life,' she responded. 'I thought you were coming yesterday.'

'I tried to ring but you didn't pick up.'

'And? You could have left a message.'

'I don't like leaving messages.'

'We all have to do things we don't like, Zuhal—but it would have been common courtesy to have informed me that you weren't going to be here when you said you were. I have to be able to rely on you. Darius is too young to know the difference right now, but in the future he needs to know that you're going to turn up when you say you are.'

He frowned, knowing that she had a point and realising that nobody—nobody—had ever spoken to him quite so caustically before. 'I had business to attend to in Paris.'

'So I saw in the papers.'

His eyes narrowed as he detected a faint crack in her voice. 'I thought you didn't read the papers.'

'I...' She seemed a little lost for words at this and swallowed, before tilting her chin with the stubborn gesture he had grown to recognise. 'Why are you here, Zuhal? If it's to see Darius then perhaps you'd like to wait in the sitting room until he's awake? If it's to organise access arrangements, then wouldn't it be better if it was done officially, through your office and your lawyers?'

He studied her. 'And that's what you want, is it?'

She swallowed again, but even so when her words came out they still sounded as if she had a foreign body lodged in her throat. 'Yes, that's what I want.'

Zuhal stilled as something inside him twisted. Something which felt like pain. Not the brutal kind, which came from a cut or a blow, but something much more insidious— and yet it was sharp. Crushingly sharp. He held his palm over his chest, as if that might steady the erratic beat of his heart as he looked into green-gold eyes which contained the hint of unshed tears.

'Jazz?' he said huskily, even though he wasn't really sure what it was he was asking.

'I'm not sure I can deal with this,' she said, with a brisk shake of her head. 'Not right now. I'm not in the mood. You told me you didn't like drama—that you saw enough of it during your childhood to put you off it for ever—well, neither do I. I wasn't expecting you and I'm not…prepared.'

'Why do you need to be prepared for my visit?'

She shook her head. 'It doesn't matter.'

'It does. It matters to me.'

Jasmine stared at him. Was he completely *stupid*? Didn't he realise that since returning she'd realised just how much he'd burrowed his way underneath her skin? That the memory of his proud hawkish features swam into her mind at pretty much every opportunity? That she missed him. She missed him more than she had any right to miss him.

But why tell him any of that? Why *should* she admit her weakness—and her love—for a man who didn't want it? That would completely disrupt the delicate balance of power which existed between them, which they needed to maintain in the future. It wasn't as if they weren't ever going to see each other again. Because of Darius there were bound to be lots of times over the years when they would bump into one another and she needed to ensure things stayed dignified and civilised between them. And that was never going to happen if Zuhal thought she was pining for him. Suddenly Jasmine could picture him laughing about her behind her back, perhaps when he was lying in bed with a new lover. Could imagine his drawled, cruel words as he dissected their relationship with forensic accuracy.

Jazz? Oh, she's nobody special. Just the mother of my child. There's nothing between us. The pregnancy was a mistake. Does she love me? She could even imagine his arrogant smile. *Yeah. I guess she does.*

Well, she wasn't going to give him that pleasure. Pointedly, she looked at her watch. 'So which is it to be, Zuhal? Either way, I need to get on, so you must excuse me. I've got someone coming over to look at some of my baby designs.'

Zuhal frowned and still he felt a burst of dark restlessness as something occurred to him. He remembered one morning when he'd found Jazz in the nursery, just before Kamal had returned. She'd been sitting on the floor flicking a balloon in front of their gurgling son, while dappled sunlight from the rose garden had streamed in on them both. She'd looked up at him and smiled, with a look of simple joy in her eyes, and he had smiled back. His heart pounded as he remembered going off to his office, whistling softly beneath his breath. He thought about the hard morning rides he'd taken since she'd gone, which had failed to work their magic, mainly because she hadn't been there to talk to. The space at the lunch table, which seemed so bare without her. The high chair which had been put away, as if Darius had never even been there.

His jaw clenched and the pain which had been twisting inside him grew unbearable. He knew he could walk away after he'd seen his little boy. He could agree that all such future meetings would probably be best conducted on neutral territory, through their respective lawyers. Or he could tell her the truth, which was only just beginning to dawn on him. A shocking truth which seemed to have come at him out of nowhere.

He thought back to when he'd discovered he had a son and told Jazz he would continue to seek a suitable bride, before blithely announcing that Darius would be his 'insurance policy' in case his new wife proved infertile. Suddenly he recognised just how wickedly cruel his words had been, though he'd never really stopped to consider the consequences of saying them before now. He thought how tolerant she had been, even in the face of all that heartlessness. How strong and brave in withstanding the undoubted suspicion and coolness of the palace servants when he'd first taken her to Razrastan. And determined, too. She had rejected his advances when they'd arrived at the royal palace—with a single-mindedness he suspected most other women wouldn't have displayed in her place. Didn't that make him respect her even more?

'Jazz, listen to me.'

'We've said everything we need to say.'

'But that's where you're wrong. I haven't even started but I need to start now by telling you just how much I miss you—'

'No!' she butted in, urgent desperation in her voice, as if she couldn't bear to hear what he was about to say. 'One thing I've always admired about you is your honesty—so please don't ruin that by telling me lies!'

'Not lies but the truth,' he argued doggedly, as the certainty inside him grew. Like when your plane dropped down, out of the cotton-wool blur of the clouds—and suddenly there was a whole clear landscape below you. 'I've realised why I ended my relationship with you the first time round—long before I planned to.'

'Don't,' she whispered, with a shake of her blonde head. 'Just *don't.*'

'It was because you used to make me *feel* stuff,' he continued, undeterred. 'Stuff I didn't want to feel. I listed all the reasons why you were unsuitable for any kind of future and I forced myself to believe them. But I never forgot you, Jazz. Not ever. Why else do you think I chose to come to you when I needed comfort and succour after my brother disappeared?'

'Because you thought I would be a walk-over?'

He shook his head. 'No,' he said simply. 'Not that. And not just because you were the best lover I've ever had but because something told me that with you I would be able to break

the rule of a lifetime, and talk. Why else did I
never...' his voice deepened, and cracked '...
take another woman to my bed, since parting
from you?'

She was staring up at him, disbelief wid-
ening her green-gold eyes. 'Are you trying to
tell me you haven't had sex with anyone else
since we split up?'

'I am telling you, because it's the truth,'
he clarified unsteadily. 'And I'll you another.
That my morning rides haven't been the same
without you by my side to talk to. That the palace has seemed empty without you there. But
I'll tell you something else, something which
eclipses all those other realisations and that
is that I love you. I love you, Jazz. I love you
so very much.'

She shook her face from side to side, her
expression disbelieving and mulish. 'But you
don't want love. You don't do love.'

'That's what I thought and that's what I
said—only now I discover I was wrong. Because I don't want to live without it. Without
you. Without Darius. My family—the most
precious thing in the world, which I almost
let slip through my fingers.' He reached out
and took her hands in his, and even though

they lay there—inert and cold—she didn't pull them away. 'Will you forgive me for all the cruel and unthinking words I've said to you, my beautiful Jazz? Will you give me another chance to show you that I am capable of change, and of love? Will you allow me to become the husband you deserve? To cherish you and protect you for as long as I live?'

There was a pause during which she shook her head again as she stared down at the exquisite silken rug he'd had shipped here from Razrastan. But when at last she lifted her gaze to his, he could see bright tears brimming over in her extraordinary eyes, making them look like new leaves which were drenched with the morning dew.

'Yes,' she whispered, at last. A tear was trickling down her cheek but her fingers were curling into his. 'How could I refuse when I love you, too? When I've never stopped loving you, no matter how hard I tried.'

He smiled but it took an effort as he realised just how close he'd come to losing her. And as he pulled her close, he discovered that the wetness on her cheek was mingling with tears of his own. 'But now you don't have to try any more, my love. The only thing you have to do right now is to seal our love in the most traditional way of all.' His words grew unsteady as he positioned her face so that her mouth was within claiming distance. 'So kiss me, Jazz. Kiss me and convince me all this is real.'

EPILOGUE

It was a perfectly warm English evening. The sinking sun was gilding the edges of the sky as dusk glimmered on the horizon. On the veranda of their large, white house overlooking green hills and rolling countryside, Jasmine kicked off her shoes, which were sinfully high to walk in, but which were her husband's undoubted favourite, which was why she wore them. Briefly, she closed her eyes because she still got a sharp hit of pleasure whenever she thought about those two words.

My husband.

The man she had married and the man she loved. The man who loved her back and who had no qualms about showing her just how much.

As if on cue, Zuhal emerged from the house where he had been kissing their three children goodnight after reading them one of the many Razrastanian fables which Jasmine was eager to see translated into English because they were just so *good*. Darius particularly liked the one about the desert falcon who discovered the lost rubies before turning into a prince and marrying the Princess. Unbelievably, their son was nearly five now and a bright tearaway who loved teasing his twin sisters, Yasmin and Anisa—eighteen months old and the apples of their father's eye.

She looked up at him and smiled. 'Everything quiet?'

Zuhal's answering smile was slow, the glint in his eyes provocative and his murmured reply contented. 'Fast asleep. Which means we have the whole evening ahead of us. What would you like to do, my love?'

What Jasmine sometimes wanted was to pinch herself, to ask herself whether this could really be happening, if life could possibly be this good. But it could, and it was. From difficult and rocky beginnings there had emerged the kind of relationship she had never imagined would exist between her and the Sheikh of Razrastan.

She and Zuhal had married in a lavish ceremony in his country, attended by the great and the good from around the globe and, in the absence of a father, his brother Kamal had consented to give her away. She had become close to the King in the time leading up to their wedding and during their subsequent visits, though, as she sometimes said to Zuhal, he had hinted at something which had happened to him during his period away from the palace—something to do with a woman, which had not yet been resolved.

And then something else wonderful had happened. Her ex-husband had seen the reports of her marriage in the newspapers and had wished her every happiness, telling her that he had remarried himself. In fact, Richard and David had managed to track down a rare, first edition of Razrastanian poems and had sent it to her and Zuhal as a wedding present and, with that simple gesture, yet another scar of the past had been healed.

As newly-weds, she and the Sheikh had decided to settle in England, moving to an enormous estate in the beautiful county of Sussex, where Zuhal had achieved a lifetime ambition and, in addition to his thriving property and shares portfolio, had opened up his own polo club, which was currently breaking all records. It had taken him a while to adjust from the idea of being a prosperous king to being a prosperous businessman again, but he had seen the many benefits his new life offered him. And these days he articulated all his hopes and fears to his beloved wife.

In the early days of the polo club, he had received practical advice from the dashing ex-player Alejandro Sabato, who had assured Jasmine that Zuhal had played no part in the photograph which had been plastered all over the press, of the two men emerging from a restaurant with several blonde women in pursuit that night in Paris.

'He was unusually quiet that night,' Alej had mused. 'And several times he mentioned your name. I knew then that he was in love with you.'

Jasmine smiled, as Zuhal walked over to her and began to massage her shoulders. In love. Yes. Her previously closed-up lover had become the most demonstrative and affectionate of men.

'You haven't answered my question,' Zuhal murmured, as he bent to kiss her neck. 'About what you'd like to do tonight?'

She turned her head a little, so that she

could catch the ebony gleam of his dark eyes. 'Any suggestions?'

'Plenty,' he murmured. 'But you are a re-markably difficult woman to please. I try to shower you with jewels, but you aren't inter-ested.'

She held up her left hand as she surveyed the rare blue stone which had been purloined from the palace vaults in Razrastan. 'That's because one diamond is enough.'

'And I offer to fly you to Paris for the week-end, but you refuse.'

'That's because there's no place like home.'

He smiled. 'You didn't even want to go out for dinner tonight, despite the fact that the chef of the restaurant I was planning to take you to has just won his third Michelin star. Which makes me wonder what exactly you would like to do tonight, my beautiful Sheikha Al Haidar?'

With a soft laugh Jasmine rose to her feet, wiggling her now bare toes against the cool tiles as she looped her arms around her hus-band's neck and planted her lips just a few centimetres away from his. 'I think I'd like to take you to bed,' she murmured. 'To show you and tell you just how much I love you, and how much I value having you in my life.'

Zuhal nodded, his throat suddenly constricting. 'And I shall tell you yet again that I became the luckiest man in the world all those days ago, when I walked into a hotel boutique and saw you standing there, blushing and not quite meeting my eyes.'

Her beautiful face was so close to his. And, as he always did in times of great emotion—which he no longer attempted to bury or deny—Zuhal used the poetic words of his native tongue, a language which Jazz was gradually coming to understand.

'If I stood you next to all the planets which glow in the mighty desert sky,' he said huskily, 'then you would be the very brightest, my darling Jazz.'

He lowered his head to hers and began to kiss her—tenderly at first, but with a fast-growing passion which soon had her moaning with pleasure. And the stars were shimmering like diamond dust in the darkening sky by the time Zuhal lifted his wife into his arms and carried her into the bedroom.

* * * * *